THE GATE OF LEMNOS

Borgo Press Books by FRANCIS JARMAN

Culture and Identity (editor)
Encountering the Other (editor)
The Gate of Lemnos: A Science Fiction Novel
Girls Will Be Girls: A Play
Intercultural Communication in Action (editor)
Invictus: A Play
Lip Service: A Play
A Star Fell: A Play
*White Skin, Dark Skin, Power, Dream: Collected
    Essays on Literature & Culture*

THE GATE OF LEMNOS

A SCIENCE FICTION NOVEL

FRANCIS JARMAN

THE BORGO PRESS

MMXI

THE GATE OF LEMNOS

FIRST EDITION

Published by Wildside Press LLC

www.wildsidebooks.com

DEDICATION

For Lucy

CONTENTS

CHAPTER ONE: In Custody 9

CHAPTER TWO: A Matter of Identity 19

CHAPTER THREE: Questions... 31

CHAPTER FOUR: The Gate of Lemnos 41

CHAPTER FIVE: ...And Interrogations 47

CHAPTER SIX: Framed 57

CHAPTER SEVEN: Don't Underestimate People . 67

CHAPTER EIGHT: The *Starstretcher* 79

CHAPTER NINE: Into the Pods 85

CHAPTER TEN: Choices Great and Small 95

CHAPTER ELEVEN: Guardian Rebek'a 109

CHAPTER TWELVE: Sqot 117

CHAPTER THIRTEEN: The Universe Is a
    Dangerous Place. 129

APPENDIX ONE: Terran Social Strata 141

APPENDIX TWO: Interstellar Transportation. . 143

ABOUT THE AUTHOR 145

"By the pricking of my thumbs,
Something wicked this way comes"

William Shakespeare, *Macbeth*

CHAPTER ONE
IN CUSTODY

BUZZ-CLICK. THE STRIP LIGHTING WENT ON. Burk was already awake, but the sudden light dazzled him. There must be a reason for switching it on. They had let him sleep—probably for hours—but now they wanted something from him.

Burk stretched, got up, and stretched again. The cell was narrow, much narrower than a single room in any of the living units, but the ceiling was high enough to allow him to stretch comfortably. This wasn't some punishment cell tucked away under the machinery deck. Those cells weren't pleasant at all. This one was on a main level, he guessed, between one of the outer gangways and the shell. He'd had time to learn the layout of the ship. He was still in the civilized world! And, sure enough, there was even a small porthole window.

He looked out, without expecting to see anything, perhaps just a blur of starlight. The ship was in slide hyperdrive. Its destination, Lemnos in the Zora System, would still be light-years away, and to reach it they would eventually need to go even faster, putting everyone into transportation pods for a final burst of interstellar high slide. So how did Burk know that the ship was only moving at slide, at normal cruising speed? Because if it wasn't, he would have fragmented into particles long ago. A very messy business, that.

Two low-ranking Guardians had come for him, both of them women, which was normal enough when it was a serious matter. He confirmed his name and number to them. They had asked him to step outside his living unit, and then some comedian had hit him from behind with a sedative taser. Was that last night? Or this morning? On a space flight, concepts like that didn't mean very much. Hours ago, certainly. The bastards! Why use a taser on him? He wouldn't have put up a fight—though in retrospect (feeling the soreness) he would have liked to—because there wouldn't have been any point. Where do you run to, on a space transporter in mid-flight? Where do you hide? And why should he need to hide anyway? He wasn't aware of having broken any serious regulations. A few recreational misdemeanors. Nothing that he thought *they* needed to know about.

With a brief whirring sound the door to the cell slid open. A Guardian stood silhouetted against the gangway, a taser of some kind in one hand and a small tray of food in the other. She was quite young, but ugly, slab-faced and expressionless. With a twist of her neck she motioned to Burk to step back. Without taking her eyes off him, she placed the tray down on the sleeping ledge.

Even if Burk hadn't seen the single red slash on her shoulder, he would have known from the coarseness of the dark green uniform and her slovenly manner and movements that she was only a Grade I—and she would likely never be anything more than that. Hers would be a life of crude, brutal service, yet also of privilege. *She* would never have her food resources withheld, *she* would never be triaged. For just a second the image of Milliya flashed through his mind: even younger, that same uniform, also Grade I, though there the resemblance ended. He repressed the thought. Milliya...it was not to be. It was painful to think of her.

Slabface went out, the door whirred shut, and Burk turned to the food tray. They were standard AdPop rations, neither better nor worse than what he had been eating and drinking since the ship left Terra. It wasn't a diet that you'd want to recommend to your dearest friends. Or serve at a party. But you got the food resources that your classification entitled you to, which was fair enough. That was the way things were. Burk was classified as Additional (not even as Useful) Population, AdPop for short, and he was certainly not a Guardian. When food resources were limited (as they frequently were), the AdPops wouldn't starve, but they couldn't expect to do much by way of feasting.

But something was wrong here. He counted the little bars and the tablets of concentrate. They had given him barely half of what he should be getting. Had they already reclassified him, then? Perhaps he was now a

SurPop, one of those convict laborers, prisoners, delinquents, addicts and social inadequates who made up the lowest rung, the Surplus Population. Some people said it would have been more honest and more realistic to call them "Superfluous". The proposal to start triaging them systematically, the repeat offenders at least, came up year after year in Parliament. So far it had always been voted down. Did SurPops routinely get less of the same food resources that the AdPops received? Or did they perhaps get the same quantity, but poorer quality stuff?

He didn't know. The strata of society weren't encouraged to mix more than was necessary—his relationship with Milliya, brief as it had been, had been very discreet—and SurPops were always trouble, there was no denying that. Burk didn't like them, he kept away from them, and he didn't know much about their official rations. Their preferred (though *unofficial*) diet was centered on what used to be called "forbidden substances", before the Government started mass-producing the stuff. In any case, on a space flight the arrangements would likely be different.

Were there any SurPops on board? Burk hadn't actually seen any. Before the Guardians had come for him, his job had taken him all round the ship and he had had plenty of contact with the crew and the passengers. The *Starstretcher* was a comfortable people transporter, of fairly new design. It had the ability to go into high slide for quite long bursts, though that did mean putting almost everyone into transportation pods, which was expensive. Lemnos needed quality settlers, though, and the *Starstretcher* was now bringing several thousand of them. SurPops (if they were needed at all—did Lemnos have mines or quarries, for instance? Or was there a convict settlement there?) could be shipped out cheaply on a non-priority freighter, some ore- or coal-transporter that never went any faster than good old S-mode, standard slide. There was no special hurry to get *them* anywhere. Making the SurPops spend a couple of years trundling through space in some discomfort and with no access to their precious "substances" could even have been designed as part of their punishment.

Burk didn't want to be a SurPop, no sirree, *anywhere* in the Terran Empire.

He nibbled at the food resources, without appetite or enthusiasm. The wrapper on the bar said "DELICIO EXTRA". Oh dear, they must be joking! Still, who knew when he might next get an even halfway decent meal? And he would need his strength. He didn't know what they wanted from him, or why the violence, but when the Guardians came for you like that, one thing was sure: it was hardly going to be a lot of fun (at least, not for you).

* * * * * * *

THEY MUST HAVE BEEN WATCHING HIM. They knew the moment Burk had finished eating, and then a whole gang of them came in for him in a rush through the whirring, sliding door. Two of them pinioned him from behind. One of them was probably a male—

Burk only caught a glimpse of them as they pushed into the cell, but he got the distinct impression that his left arm was being pinioned by someone less thuggish than the Guardian who was trying to break his right arm (despite their smaller size, the females tended to be more brutal). There was quite a crowd of them in the little cell. Burk must have done something to make himself a celebrity! Slabface was there, too, standing in the background, poised on her toes and looking as though she was simply dying to cause him grievous bodily harm, in an expert and enthusiastic manner, if only her colleagues would step aside for a moment and give her the opportunity to demonstrate her skills. A nasty-looking Grade II (two red slashes) did all the talking, or what there was of it.

"You've 'ad yer food. Now you're gonna answer some questions!"

And before he could respond they bundled him out of the cell, down the gangway, round several corners, through a couple of sliding doors and into a room with a numbered but otherwise unmarked dark green door. On the way, Cruella had squawked "Move it! Yer! Move it! Go! Go!" or something similarly theatrical that she had picked up from lousy old twenty-first century movies. She had also kicked his shins in a perfunctory, Guardian-like way. Perhaps she thought she was up for a promotion, and her superiors were watching? How had she even got to Grade II, with language skills like that?

They went past numerous people, all of them in

Guardian uniforms. No attempt was made to disorientate him or hide from him where they were going. They were on the lower administration level of the ship, the door-numbers had told him that. There were larger porthole windows in the gangway, through which he now saw clear starlight. That meant that, for some reason, the ship was completely out of slide and had slowed down to T- (or "terrestrial") speed. It was good to know that they were in a public area of the *Starstretcher*. If they had been planning to do him serious harm, some interrogation *off the record*, or worse, they would have taken him somewhere else on the ship. Somewhere that was much darker and quieter.

The room they were now in was a medium-sized office, with tables, chairs, and all the usual paraphernalia of administration. Lots of communications stuff, but no obvious instruments for inflicting pain, Burk thought to himself. Except the fists, boots and tasers of the Guardians, of course, which were always available.

"Sit there!" Cruella pushed him down onto a simple office chair. Burk was aware of her standing behind him, breathing heavily and shifting her weight from foot to foot. She smelt distinctly unpleasant. She's nervous! Maybe she really was under supervision for promotion. Or was she simply *frightened* of the other people in the room? Her thuggish colleagues were now gone, or so Burk thought, though he didn't want to risk looking round to find out. Instead, he focused on who was sitting in front of him.

They had done him proud: no fewer than three Grade

IIIs—the officer class. The uniforms were nicely cut, clean and well-fitting. Directly opposite him sat a fairly young woman with a sternly beautiful face and a look of high but cold intelligence. Burk was immediately reminded of lines from a Yeats poem:

Pallas Athene in that straight back and arrogant head
All the Olympians; a thing never known again.

(Minor subject Literature at college—it had to be good for *something*.)

On the table in front of her was a bulky dossier with assorted printouts of texts, reports and graphics. Could that be his Main File? He couldn't see exactly. Whatever the matter was about, it must be serious. Paper was much heavier than electronically stored information. On a crowded people transporter it was a luxury, a valuable resource. Burk remembered the fuss they'd made about the couple of old-fashioned books that he'd included in his luggage. Most things were digitalized for text-readers long ago, but he liked to be holding a proper book in his hands when he read his favorite poets. Athene played with the items, ignoring Burk for the moment.

To her left was a male officer, older than she was, more delicately built, with long, thin artistic hands and a slightly distant expression. He looked vaguely familiar. Burk had once been told, by someone who had painfully good cause to know, that senior Guardian interrogators, the ones who did the more *subtle*, the more *complicatedly unpleasant* things to you, often looked like this. And they always smiled while they were doing it. Suddenly the man became aware of Burk, and stared at him in an amused manner. (Though whether the thought that was amusing him would have amused Burk, too, would be rather hard to say.)

The third officer sat away from the table, to her female colleague's right, as though she were only there as an observer. She was the highest in rank. In addition to the three red slashes, there were two red stars, indicating that she was only one promotion away from Grade IV, the junior leadership cadre—the highest level that was normally allowed to leave Terra, and then only to assume command. If she was being posted to Lemnos on a permanent basis, rather than to carry out a specific and temporary mission, only the Governor of the planet would outrank her, with the military commander and the security chief perhaps her equals in rank. Nobody on the *Starstretcher* would outrank her, though, except the Commander.

She was also the most physically intimidating of the three Guardians. Her massive body caused the uniform to bulge. She had huge hands, ideal for mending metal bars or cracking open Goro-nuts without a hammer. There was nothing about her figure, as far as Burk could see, that proclaimed incontrovertibly that she was a woman (she didn't seem to have breasts, for example). Although she was physically impressive, even attractive (in an androgynous way), she couldn't be an android, because they were not admitted into the ranks of the Guardians. Perhaps she had been genetically modified or enhanced?

Guardians were not allowed to wear jewelry *on* duty (or encouraged to wear it *off*), but some of them—Burk thought for a heart-warming second of Milliya—managed to customize their uniforms with discreet little feminine touches. No such touches were evident here. Only two things suggested her sex.

One was the way that her hair was done, in an unmistakably female style, with patient care and immaculate taste, and undoubtedly at great expense.

The other was the Medusa-like gaze that she fixed on Burk when their eyes finally met, a look that told him that here was a woman who had had dealings with men before, and who had her own very personal reasons for wanting to wield power over them, to humiliate them, and to cause them pain.

It was a look that chilled him to the bone.

CHAPTER TWO
A MATTER OF IDENTITY

"Do let me apologize," the Goddess rather unexpectedly began, "for the, er, *robust* way that you have been treated. It is connected with the nature of the charges against you. Our lower-grade colleagues are good-hearted but simple people"—Burk thought he heard Cruella behind him grunt ever so slightly—"who, confronted with behavior of a particularly despicable kind, find it difficult not to give vent to their feelings in a direct and physical manner. We don't condone that, but we can understand it."

She paused, then looked down at one of the papers in front of her.

"I have here a Form 26a, if you wish to make a complaint?"

That too had been printed out!

Burk shrugged. It was widely believed that asking for Form 26a could easily led to Form 27b being needed soon afterwards, and with no detour that took in Forms 26b ("Verification of Complaint by Interrogating Officer"), 26c ("Staff Affidavit / Complaints"), 26d ("Witness Statement / Complaints") or 27a ("Mental or Physical Heath Issues during Interrogation"). Form 27b was the one that documented the details of an "Accidental Fatality during Interrogation".

She looked up again.

"No?" Form 26a was put to one side. "It remains your right, of course, to register a complaint at any time during this meeting if you believe that someone has overstepped the mark. Do you understand that?"

"Yes, of course."

"Then perhaps we should get down to business. I am Guardian Grade III Sousanna, from Crime and Security. I will be leading this investigation."

Guardians were always referred to by their first name, as if that in some inexplicable way made them nicer.

She nodded in the direction of her effeminate male colleague.

"This is Guardian Grade III Adriyan, from the administration."

Adriyan leaned forward towards Burk, with an insinuating smile.

"I believe that we've already met?"

"I don't think so."

"At the Commander's dinner, the night after we launched from Terra? Before we went into the pods for high slide out of the solar system? We were at the same table. Surely you remember?"

Burk *did* remember him after all, though they had barely spoken to each other. Guardian Adriyan had spent most of that evening chatting up a handsome crewman, whom he obviously found more interesting. That had been fine with Burk: he had sat nursing his drink, desperately unhappy, trying not to think of Milliya and almost looking forward to a couple of light-years of unconsciousness in the pod.

"Yes, I do remember now."

"Colleague Adriyan is in the Social and Recreational Department. Which is why he is taking part in our enquiry, you understand."

Logical enough, since that was the section that Burk worked in on the *Starstretcher* (although he'd had no further contact with winsome Colleague Adriyan); otherwise, unfortunately, Burk didn't understand at all. However, what he *had* noticed was Guardian Sousanna's apparent unwillingness to use the ominous word "interrogation". Which could only be a good sign, he thought.

"And this is Guardian Grade III (Senior Level) Rebek'a. From Ideology."

She gestured politely towards her huge colleague, who acknowledged the gesture by turning her basilisk gaze on Burk.

"It is slightly unusual to have someone of her rank participating in an initial procedure of this kind, but it was felt that the investigation would benefit from her experience and expertise."

Oh yes, Burk thought, looking at the huge fore-arms and muscular neck. I wonder what her special area of expertise just happens to be? At which point she smiled, a smile which made Guardian Sousanna or even Slabface look like an angel of mercy, and said quietly:

"Now we want to know who *you* are, little man."

She had a deep voice, and spoke in the measured tone of someone who was used to being obeyed.

Before Burk could answer that, Guardian Sousanna rustled the papers in front of her, cleared her throat, and began to speak.

"Burk, John. No further names. Thirty years old. Birthplace, parents, nothing of particular interest there."

Guardian Adriyan interrupted her.

"'John' is spelled in the old-fashioned way. *That's* interesting, I would say. Indicative perhaps of an unconventional, rebellious family background?"

Guardian Rebek'a: "Or that he had stupid parents?"

"Well, yes, Colleague, it would be stupid behavior in the sense that it would draw attention to the boy in later life, and for no good reason."

"He could have changed his name, though. But he didn't. Perhaps our friend *wanted* to be seen as a non-conformist. A sentimental traditionalist. Out of step with the established order of things in our modern universe. *A trouble-maker.*"

"Colleagues, colleagues...." Guardian Sousanna was now visibly exasperated. "This sort of speculation isn't very helpful. I'd like to continue if I may?"

Her colleagues both nodded.

"Very well. *School.* Regarded as intelligent but unconventional. Media Studies at college. Minor in

Literature. Pretty straightforward stuff."

Now all three of the Guardians snorted. And they were right, of course. Burk's college had been famous, but only for its fantastic social scene, and Media Studies was a notoriously cushy option. Career Guardians, on the other hand, tended to study useful subjects like Advanced Cybernetics, Inormation Technology or Administration. Or Ideological Theory. Or Politics and Law.

"Good but not exactly spectacular grades. No application was submitted for Guardian training, despite recommendations made by the school *and* by the university. Interesting, that…. Various jobs, journalism, public relations, including the present posting to the *Starstretcher*. A few run-ins with the Government censor. No *excessively* long periods of unemployment, given his rather unpromising qualification profile."

She paused.

"Quite good references. For the most part."

She wasn't reading, but extrapolating the relevant information from the documents. What could they be looking for? What would be "of particular interest" to them?

At this point Guardian Adriyan chimed in with: "Are you related to Ciaran Burke?"

Pause.

Burk feigned ignorance, pretending to be racking his brains.

"You mean: Kieran Bourke the football player?" (Though it was Kieran *Brake*, as he well knew.)

"No, I don't mean Kieran Bourke the football player. I mean Ciaran Burke the terrorist."

Guardian Adriyan was clearly a history buff. Ciaran Burke ("the terrorist") had organized what little resistance there was to the mass triaging in Africa during the last great Water Crisis. Burk—no relation—hardly thought of him as a terrorist. Dr. Ciaran was an obsessional, unstable idealist, a man of noble intentions and zero effectiveness who had come to a predictably sticky end. Not a person that Burk would normally want to find himself associated with.

"No. And it's Burk without an 'E'."

In his recreation hours, Burk had researched high and low in the genealogical archives, hoping to find a "Burke" in the family, more aristocratic, more intellectual-sounding, more *Irish* than just plain "Burk", but he could only come up with Buerks, Börks and similar plebian variants.

"Burk is classified as AdPop, Lower Executive Level. Various minor entitlements, but no particular priority rating that we need to take into account. Private life: no partner or known long-term relationship. At least, not according to his file. Off the record, however—we know that he puts himself about in a rather tasteless and inappropriate manner."

"Really?"

Guardian Adriyan was all interest. Guardian Rebek'a gave him a withering look.

"But not in your direction, darling!"

Then she turned to Burk, leaning forward to give

her words more intensity.

"You're a good-looking boy, John. *Very* good-looking, in fact, albeit in a rather predictable way. I expect that you've always been able to find some poor little low-grade to rut with. I don't find that as disturbing as Colleague Sousanna here seems to. However, what does interest me is this: with your job and salary, your physique, good genes no doubt, too, why haven't you ever been chosen as a Consort?"

She laughed nastily.

"Or could it be that you're programmed like my sweet Colleague Adriyan here?"

More rustling of papers, as Guardian Sousanna looked through the information on Burk that was spread out in front of her.

"There is indeed no indication in Burk's record of an application for Consort status ever having been submitted."

Consorts were the males chosen as breeding partners by the females who made up the "useful" part of the Useful Population. Since fertilization by synthetic sperm was the normal procedure, and had been for more than a century, Consorts—who were given honorary UsePop status—were males who had something very special to offer as a reason for bringing them in to fulfill what was, after all, an outdated and superfluous procreative role. Perhaps charm, or looks, intelligence, sexual sophistication, excellent parenting or home-making skills, any or all of those qualities. Whatever it was, a Consort would need to have it in spades to make some Breeder prefer his sexual company to that of a pleasure android.

"No Breeder seems to have noticed him, though."

"And he is not (as far as I can tell) 'programmed' like myself, as you so charmingly put it." He tittered slightly. "*Unfortunately*, I would even go so far as to add. But one always lives in hope, I like to think."

Burk remembered how crudely Guardian Adriyan had eyed him up at the reception. Receiving no encouraging body-language signals in reply, he had quickly transferred his attention to the crewman, Dhavid, a lad who was well known on the ship for putting out with lusty enthusiasm to alpha males who were that way inclined.

"So, John doesn't particularly go for girls *or* boys, then? Well, well!"

Burk didn't much like the way Guardian Rebek'a used his first name.

"The documentation that we have on Burk is still incomplete. Much of this information, additional to the personnel material that was in his shipboard file, had to be extracted from his Main File and transmitted from Terra. As you can imagine, the communication channels on a people transporter in interstellar slide tend to be choked with transmission data, and the present investigation is, after all, hardly a matter of high priority."

"I beg to disagree. John is very high priority with *me*, Colleague."

"What do you mean by that? If you have any information that you are withholding from this investigation, Colleague...."

"I am authorized to withhold whatever I like, as you well know."

"True. But let me remind you that I am the officer in charge of this investigation."

"There are some matters that your rank doesn't qualify you to investigate, Colleague."

"Don't forget that you are here on my initiative. As a gesture of politeness."

"And we will all be very polite to each other," it seemed to Burk that that probably didn't include *him*, "although I am here because I was sent here, and I will tell you what you need to know when you need to know it. At the appropriate time. *Colleague*."

The two women were now glaring at each other, bristling (or the nearest thing to bristling that women can manage) and breathing heavily. Burk wouldn't normally have backed anyone against Guardian Rebek'a, who was just about the most fearsome human specimen he had ever seen. But there was something hard and determined about Guardian Sousanna—here was a woman who wouldn't back down easily if she believed that she was in the right.

Hey, this is almost fun, he thought. Apart from the tasering of course. More importantly, by losing their cool the Guardians were dropping hints about things that he desperately wanted to know. Such as—what was this whole business all about? Why did he have to be locked up, shouted at and frogmarched around like a SurPop addict with withdrawal symptoms? What "particularly despicable" thing was it that he was supposed to have done?

To keep it all going, he thought, what would now be ideal would be for some mere man to stick his oar in, and, sure enough, this is exactly what happened. Before Burk himself could think of anything clever to say, Guardian Adriyan decided to join in the action.

"Ladies, ladies, please."

CLANG! Disaster! The two female Guardians rounded on their colleague in fury. He couldn't have chosen his words worse if he had tried. "Ladies" was the contemptuous, euphemistic term that (female) Guardians used for female AdPops (just as useless AdPop males like Burk were referred to sneeringly as "Drones"). Burk couldn't help smiling. Had dear Adriyan been dozing when they covered these topics in the Interactive Skills module of his Guardian training?

At this point there should really have been a three-way rough-house between the Guardians, which would have been most entertaining to watch! But it never even started, because quite suddenly all hell broke loose.

The ship's alarm sirens went off, and the lighting began to pulsate in sync with the alarm. Feet pounded in the gangway outside. Loud voices shouted excitedly. All three Guardians at once withdrew into themselves, completely ignoring each other—and Burk. Eyes narrowed, hunched and deathly still, they concentrated on the messages that were already being channeled through to them on the personal communicators attached to their wrists. Other messages—doubtless with the same information—were probably flickering on the screens in front of them.

Guardian Sousanna motioned to Cruella, or whoever it was who was standing behind Burk. "Get him out of here! Now!"

A few seconds later, Burk was knocked out by a sedative taser. But just before he felt the shock, he heard one of the three Guardians say, to the others, not to him, and in a voice of dumbfounded amazement: "This can't be happening! The ship is under attack!"

CHAPTER THREE
QUESTIONS...

WHEN BURK EVENTUALLY CAME TO, the thought that flashed through his mind was the same sensational, unthinkable one that he had before he was tasered for the second time that day. The ship is under attack? *By whom?*

There were no longer any pirates in the Terran Empire. Sure, there had been once, during the Troubled Times, but they had only attacked slow, low-priority freighters, and not always with success. Ciaran Burke's brief career had included a certain amount of piracy, as he attempted to embarrass the Empire by highjacking valuable resources. But an attack on a fast, modern people transporter, a ship bristling with security Guardians and military personnel, would have been unthinkable.

And if it wasn't pirates? No life-forms more advanced than microbes had so far been encountered in the parts of the universe that were known to the Terrans, except in the remote corner that was the *Starstretcher*'s current destination. Lemnos was unlikely to be the source of the danger, though. The vegetation that covered most of that planet—the ubiquitous, mysterious moss called *sqot*, the oh so delicious but unfortunately also very rare (and expensive) Goro-nuts, the stringy-looking, foul-smelling ferns, the edible but boring Lemnian bananas, normally fed only to livestock and convicts—none of this stuff was likely to have an aggressive military agenda. There would be no "Lemnian War" between the human race and alien vegetables!

Could the settlers have rebelled? But why should they? Lemnos was absolutely *the* most attractive posting in the Empire, now increasingly so as Terra became ever more disgustingly polluted. On Lemnos (Burk had been told) you could still see the planet's star, Zora, rise and set. On Terra, you could only tell where Helios was from the dull radiance glowing behind a section of the dense clouds of smog and muck.

Even if the settlers were up in arms for some strange reason, what ship could they use for pirate attacks? There were always freighters and (less often) transporters coming and going, but nothing as sophisticated as the *Starstretcher* had ever been to Lemnos before, and (to the best of Burk's knowledge) no battle cruisers or fighters were presently stationed there. Also: Burk was an information officer. If anything sensational had actually happened on Lemnos, Burk would have heard at least a rumor of it. As he had, in fact, already acquired all kinds of information about the planet, most of the items rather disquieting, from a range of sources, including Milliya.

If there had been a full-scale rebellion, wouldn't she

have known?

His body ached from the tasering, and the sleeping ledge was distinctly uncomfortable, but so were the thoughts going through Burk's mind. One in particular. If the *Starstretcher* hadn't been under attack by any known force from within the Terran Empire, did that mean that the attackers had come from outside? Could this be the famous moment of "first contact", the initial encounter with an alien intelligence from some unimaginably distant galaxy? Burk might just have been a witness to the most significant event in human history, more important than the invention of the wheel, the discovery of America, the first moon-landing or the development of slide hyperdrive technology.

He slid off the sleeping ledge and peered out through the little porthole. The ship was back in S-mode, at cruising speed, but if they had been desperately trying to outrun attackers the *Starstretcher* would now surely be in high slide and they would all—except for the team up on the control deck—be tucked away in transportation pods. When the attack occurred, they had been quietly trundling along at T-speed, probably to enable a better transmission of data from Terra, and that had made them vulnerable.

Burk was puzzled. Had there really been an attack? Could it have been a misunderstanding? Asteroids? A freak radiation field? Hardly likely. Burk had met the Commander several times, and he was a man who inspired confidence, not one who made elementary mistakes. They wouldn't have put an incompetent in charge of an expensive prestige item like the *Starstretcher*. There were only a handful of Starreacher Class people transporters in the Imperial Fleet, and competition for the command positions was fierce. (It was Burk's job to know things like that.) Fleet Commanders were an élite corps, the only high-status professional group still dominated by men.

Had they been testing emergency procedures? Was it some sort of war game? Or: had the whole thing been staged for his benefit? Burk had a very healthy level of self-esteem—an *unhealthy* level, the Guardians would probably say, for an AdPop—but he couldn't believe that such an elaborate charade would be organized just for him. In any case: *why* go to all that trouble?

He had noticed that the three interrogators had different interests and (so it seemed to him) different degrees of knowledge. Guardian Rebek'a was out of step with her two colleagues, she knew more than they did, and she outranked them, but she wasn't in charge. If there was any trickery going on, it would probably be Rebek'a who was the instigator. Would she be able to set off the ship's alarm sirens, though, without the direct involvement of the Commander?

Whatever his actual rank (and it would be equal to hers, if not higher), it was the Commander who was in sole charge of the operation of the ship. And he was the only person on board whose operational decisions could not be countermanded, even by a high-level Guardian from the dreaded Ideology section. Faking a major alarm within a complex technical system like the *Starstretcher* would entail considerable risk, and even if the Commander had been given sealed orders to cooperate with Guardian Rebek'a, he would know that this was not unconditional and that he would be expected to use his better judgement (and assert his higher rank) whenever needed. The safety of the ship would always have priority. If it came to a conflict, he would have powerful supporters. The Federation of Fleet Officers had great political clout, and Guardian Rebek'a's superiors, whoever they were, would think twice about challenging them.

Something very strange was going on, and Burk, gazing out through the porthole at the blurred starlight, realized that he was right in the middle of it.

The door whirred open. He didn't bother to turn round. Slabface would be bringing more rations, even though he hadn't finished off what was on the tray.

"You can take the other stuff away. Just leave me the drink, please."

"So you don't like our catering, sir?"

It was a voice that he hadn't forgotten, a voice that he would never, ever, forget. Milliyas's voice.

* * * * * * *

BEFORE HE COULD SAY ANYTHING, she made the familiar Guardian command signal "Silence!", turned to check that the door to the cell had already closed behind her, and motioned to him to sit on the sleeping ledge.

"Milliya!"

"No! Stay sitting! And don't try to touch me!"

Then her voice lightened.

"No, it's not what you think, darling—at this moment there is truly nothing I would *more* like to do than kiss you!"

She tossed her bob of dark hazelnut hair, and her pretty olive face lit up with affection.

"But if they've regraded you as a prisoner you may have been tagged. And I might have to go through a control scanner later on. If they discover that I've touched the dangerous suspect," she tilted her head to a quizzical angle and gave him a wicked grin, "they might start to ask exactly *why*. Now, I may be on this ship officially, but I'm 'Guardian Jo-anna', not Guardian Milliya."

"Was it you who set off the alarm sirens?"

"Now don't be silly! I have many gifts, but they don't extend that far."

"So the alarm was real?"

"Ssh! I truly don't know, and we haven't got time for that now. I'm here to warn you. Whether I can *help* you I don't know yet. Listen! We've only got a few moments. They'll be coming to collect you, very soon. You've been set up. I'm not sure by whom. It's connected with what I told you about Lemnos, and what I asked you to do for me. I shouldn't have asked you, I know, but it's too late now. There'll be a hearing. There will be charges against you, accusations, I don't know exactly what."

"But I haven't done anything! Well, not yet I

haven't…."

"Yes, I know. It's a frame-up." She chuckled. "But you deserve all the punishment that's coming to you, my sweetheart—a good hard spanking I hope, preferably administered by me—because you were always stronger on promises than on actions!"

Their eyes met.

"No, you know I don't mean that. And my feelings for you have not changed one bit. But there are other people who know that, very powerful, very dangerous people. That's why I can't be on this ship as Guardian Milliya. And because these people don't know that I'm here, and can't hurt me (or so they think), they've made *you* their target."

"This hearing…."

"…will be strictly within the rules. They'll keep to the law. The Commander is an honest man. He wouldn't allow it to be otherwise. But they don't want you to leave the ship. And they won't let you land on Lemnos."

"Because of what you told me? About *sqot*?"

"Yes, that must be the reason. But they work in the shadows, and it's hard to see what they are doing. One thing is certain: you, my darling, are in great danger because of me, and I wouldn't want you to be hurt."

Burk smiled. He was bigger and physically much stronger than she was (although he hadn't been trained to use deadly weapons, or to kill or maim with his bare hands, as she had been), yet the way she spoke to him made him sound like a wimp who needed protection.

There was nothing personal in this. In the course of the twenty-first century the power balance between men and women had first of all become more equal and then, especially after synthetic fertilization replaced sexual intercourse as the normal method for starting procreation, had tipped over completely to the advantage of women. Officially, and legally, there was equality between the sexes, and men still held many figurehead positions, especially in public service. The Emperor was a man (of sorts), and on the Imperial Advisory Council there were as many male as female members, but women dominated the Government. In fact, in most areas of life it was women who held the key positions of power and who had the say.

A natural consequence of this was that women were often in a position to bully and harry the menfolk, and many of them indeed did so. They dressed and behaved like "power women". The way they spoke reflected this, and the discourse of communication between women and men, both their speech and their non-verbal communication, had changed radically. What used once to be thought of as "typically feminine behavior", for instance coyness and flirtatiousness, had not disappeared altogether, but it was now definitely something that could be turned on, like a tap, whenever male acquiescence was required, and then turned off again soon afterwards. (But hadn't it always been like that? Burk thought to himself.)

Milliya wasn't trying to patronize him by talking in such a way. True, she had initiated their relationship, as women mostly did, but they had soon discovered, in the brief time that they were together, that their clandestine affair—Guardians were encouraged to pair up only with each other, at least if they wanted their careers to blossom—was a well-balanced and affectionate partnership, in which, so Burk liked to think, they could be honest with each other despite the barrier of social difference.

"I got you into this." She repeated: "I don't want you to get hurt."

Before he could think of anything suitably brave, upbeat and masculine to say in reply, she was already at the door, preparing to key in a Guardian code on the control pad.

"They must make some sort of move before we reach the Gate of Lemnos. After that, the chances will be more even. They can't allow you past the Gate. Dead or alive, they'll try to keep you on this ship."

"Will they try and make me talk?"

"Yes, of course they will, but you don't really know anything that they don't already know. Except that I'm on the *Starstretcher* too. And they're not looking for me, darling. They haven't even bothered to mike this cell."

"And *why* aren't they looking for you?"

"Because they have good reason to believe that I'm dead."

It took a moment for him to grasp the implications of what she was saying.

"Yes, those are the sort of people we're dealing

with."

"How did you become 'Guardian Jo-anna'?"

"No time for that now. Let's just say that, where poor little Jo-anna has gone, she won't be needing her identity any more."

Milliya reached up to the control pad.

"Watch your back. I'll try to help you. If I can't, you'll have to do it yourself. You're a big boy now! Remember: the Gate of Lemnos is the key."

She typed in the number-code, the door whirred open, and she was gone.

CHAPTER FOUR
THE GATE OF LEMNOS

THE GATE OF LEMNOS WASN'T A GATE. It wasn't, physically, any sort of door at all, but it was an entry point. It was an area of empty space just beyond the Kallipygian moons of Lemnos where an orbiting control vessel of the Planetary Governorate passed through, docking with incoming transporters and allowing passengers to disembark, be processed, and then transferred down to the planet by shuttle. (And a similar process in the other direction, naturally.) This much Burk had gleaned from his information monitor on Terra after the booking of his flight to Lemnos had been confirmed.

There had been more, much more, about the natural beauty of the Gate. About the spectacular light effects created by Zora striking one, or the other, of the two moons of Lemnos, with the rich, dark-green surface of the planet itself shimmering seductively below. "One of the Seven Wonders of the Universe", "The most beautiful spacescape in the galaxy", and so on.

These florid, touristic descriptions dated back to an earlier time when Lemnos was still being developed for settlement. Back then, very few Terrans had been keen to go on the long, possibly dangerous and, for most of them, one-way space voyage out to the very edge of the Empire. Slide technology had not yet been perfected, the ships were fairly slow and uncomfortable, and there was a widespread suspicion that Lemnos was being developed as a large-scale dumping ground for SurPops.

"A galactic version of Botany Bay," one of Burk's schoolteachers had said, with a smug smile. It was a reference that no-one in the class had understood, and that only Burk had bothered to check out on his monitor. (For the clever-dick teacher, it may have been one witty piece of sarcasm too many, because soon afterwards he disappeared from the school, very suddenly and in the middle of the term, never to return.)

Things had changed enormously since then. Lemnos was now a very popular destination indeed, with long waiting-lists for would-be settlers, but no great effort had been made to bring the texts up to date.

Unfortunately, Burk had found scarcely any information about the customs arrangements, identity checks and security controls at the Gate—which is what he most needed to know. Milliya had said that she believed it was stricter on the way back than for incomings, and this was confirmed by the tiny number of people who *did* return from Lemnos, and by a couple of starship crew-members whom Burk had chanced to meet while he was doing a documedia report on the Imperial Fleet.

Terra had been spreading its junk galaxy-wide for

a century now, polluting every planet that it discovered, and the customs officers on the various moon and planet settlements and space stations were not especially curious about what weird rubbish people might have in their bags and boxes (they'd seen it all before), so long as it didn't weigh much. (Books were not appreciated.) They *were* seriously interested in stopping you from smuggling in weapons that might get into the hands of SurPop convicts (a messy scenario that had already been played out in numerous locations). Drugs, on the other hand, had long ceased to be an issue—the Government had a monopoly, producing and distributing them far more efficiently than anyone else could. No, customs, Burk imagined, would not be too much of a problem.

His identity would certainly be checked, but probably only cursorily, since it was assumed that if you had been enabled (by the Terran Government) to make the long and expensive voyage, and had come of your own free will, you would be a welcome addition. The settler population of Lemnos had not yet reached a critical mass. During the pioneer phase, the lavish new hospital had failed to install with sufficient care the complicated technology that was required for synthetic fertilization. There had therefore been no population explosion among the settlers, Lemnos still needed incomings, there were plenty of applications, and the Governorate had no wish to discourage new citizens with tiresome entry formalities.

Finally, there was a practical consideration that

might work to Burk's advantage. Since there were far more incomings than returnees, the overworked staff on the control vessel had apparently gotten into the habit of taking more time over the latter, thereby allowing themselves to maintain the pleasant illusion that the work they were doing was somehow important, rather than essentially just an advanced form of cattle-herding.

Because, as far as the incomings were concerned, it really was more like a stampede—the identity checks could never be more than superficial, if the incomings were to be loaded into the shuttles before these missed the narrow time window for the transfer flight to the surface of the planet. (There was no room to keep large numbers of people on the control vessel for a complete orbit of Lemnos, so if the shuttles *did* miss their window the incomings would have to be shunted back onto the transporter and the whole sequence repeated later—not a popular procedure with anyone who was involved.)

The fact that the *Starstretcher* would be docking for the very first time, a different type and size of ship than they were used to at the Gate, would no doubt also help.

All that was decidedly in his favor. What *could* possibly turn out to be awkward was the security scan, Burk thought, especially if he had been registered as someone who was under arrest or interrogation. That *would* show up. And Milliya had good reason to be nervous, too. However, so far everything had been done very informally. There had been no proper hearing, just the short, dramatically interrupted, meeting with the three Guardians. No charge, he guessed, had yet been made. What was his current status in the system then?

Shipboard arrangements were apparently more casual than procedures on Terra. Transmissions of information between Terra, the *Starstretcher*, and Lemnos would not necessarily be very efficient. If he could avoid formal charges, let alone conviction, or be released, there might be a chance for him to slip through the Gate as Milliya hoped.

If things took a turn for the worse, and he was obliged to try to escape from custody, it would become more complicated—and they might need to think up a new strategy for getting him through security. Once on the surface of Lemnos, though, he'd take his chances.

The greatest danger, however, might be from someone on board the ship. Someone who had been given the job of dealing with Burk, informally if need be, but *permanently*.

CHAPTER FIVE
...AND INTERROGATIONS

MILLIYA'S TIMING HAD BEEN GOOD. Burk had only been alone for a few minutes when Cruella and her team came to fetch him. This time there was no violence or shouting as they trundled him—manhandled wouldn't be the right word, not this time—back to the interrogation room.

Here he found himself facing the same three Guardians, sitting in the same places as before, but with a more subdued air (had something serious happened?), and with the addition of a lowly scribe, presumably there to keep a record of the hearing. How strange, Burk thought, that they're not relying on recordings or electronic minutes. Aha! It seems that someone doesn't want this information fed into the system! This could be all to the good when it came to him having to slip through the security controls at the Gate.

The scribe was a miserable, hunched little figure of a man, a low-grade AdPop no doubt terrified of the three Guardians.

Guardian Sousanna told Cruella that the escort should leave, but hold themselves in readiness to escort the prisoner back to his quarters.

Then, giving Burk a stern look, she opened the meeting.

"This is not a formal procedure. No official transcript will be made. The notes" (she pointed to the notepad held by the little clerk) "are being taken solely for our convenience. It's an informal hearing. Because of that, you don't need legal representation and you won't be offered any. That will, however, be the case, in both instances, if we decide that the matter needs to be taken further. Do you understand?"

God! Burk said to himself, using an expletive that had almost become extinct on Terra, she really does look like Pallas Athene! A superb woman. Flawlessly beautiful, and perfectly proportioned. But she was not someone that you could hope to love without being destroyed.

"Yes, of course."

Guardian Rebek'a laughed.

"You're not stupid, so I think we can talk openly. You've probably worked it all out for yourself anyway. No, Colleague"—responding dismissively to a gesture of protest from Guardian Adriyan—"he's not naïve, our little Burk. He knows that there's been an *incident*. And because of that incident the ship is going into high slide sooner than expected. It's those lovely pods for all of us! That means, sweetheart, that we don't have too much time."

It was unclear to Burk whether she was addressing Guardian Adriyan or himself. She continued—

"Our passenger list may well be crawling with lawyers, any of them happy to play the defense attorney, especially if they can spin it out into a nice long expensive hearing, but that's not going to happen. So—just an informal hearing."

"Thank you, Colleague Rebek'a, for that clarification. As I said before, all that we need to ascertain is whether this matter needs to be taken further. There is very little time available, so let me get to the point."

She turned to Burk.

"What is the nature of your present posting?"

"I have a short-term contract with the Social and Recreational Department here on the *Starstretcher*. As Guardian Adriyan knows only too well."

"But we haven't worked together, have we, Burk? And I'm not responsible for your section. Or for your actions."

Guardian Adriyan's tone was slightly indignant, as if to say that he personally wouldn't be seen dead doing whatever it was that Burk was supposed to have done.

"Thank you, Colleague, we'll come to that in more detail shortly."

Pause.

"You have a return ticket, but with no date for the return journey specified? Which means—"

"That I shall be spending some time on Lemnos, but that I do intend to return to Terra, perhaps in six or nine months, when the next transporter comes out. I'm not a settler. Is there some kind of a problem? The ships aren't usually full up on the return journey, so

I've heard."

Guardian Rebek'a laughed nastily.

"You won't be spending time on Lemnos! Not if you value your life. When the settlers hear about you, they'll tear you to pieces. If we keep you locked up, you nasty little man, we'll be doing you a favor!"

"Thank you, Colleague, but I really think that we should take this step by step!"

Burk had no idea what they were talking about, but now he was going to find out.

"One of your professional duties has been to encourage the passengers to use the recreational facilities of the *Starstretcher*. Am I correct?"

"Yes."

"This has included designing announcements and advertising images that were sent to the passengers' portable or temporary information monitors."

"Yes."

"And you were even authorized to print up a small number of flyers for passengers who are without monitor capability." (That would be the AdPops in the cheaper cabins.)

"Yes."

"Like this one, for the Water Paradise?"

She handed Burk a large information leaflet.

"Yes, that's one that I designed. But it was never used because the Water Paradise remained closed, as we all know, for technical reasons. In fact, they're still doing repairs."

"That's not to the point. Please describe to us the

image on this flyer."

"Well, there's a child, ten or eleven years old, hurtling towards you down a water chute. Looking pretty excited. It was a difficult image to get right. Lots of water splashing around."

"Since the Water Paradise on the ship never opened, how did you manage to make the image?"

"I admit I cheated a bit. It's an image that I originally made back on Terra, where I had a municipal job in a recreational center doing much the same sort of stuff. I put in a different background, though, to make it look like our Water Paradise. Hey, is this what I'm being accused of here: digital manipulation? Or of some sort of fraud? This is standard journalism, standard public relations, you know that surely?"

"No. That is not what concerns us here."

Pause.

"Look at the image of the child."

"Yes?"

"The child is *naked*."

In a flash, it dawned on Burk what they were trying to pin on him. This had to be stopped.

"No, the image of the child is cut off at the waist, obscured by the front of the chute. And the kid was wearing swimming trunks anyway."

"But we can't know that, can we? The image suggests nakedness. It stimulates people to imagine a naked child. It even invites people to imagine *you* having an intimate photo session with a naked child. Perhaps you did have such a session! That sounds pornographic to me. Burk, I have to ask you: are you a pedophile?"

Burk didn't know whether to laugh or scream.

"I Most Certainly Bloody Well Am Not!"

Guardian Rebek'a snorted, Guardian Adriyan sniggered, but the eyes of Pallas Athene flashed.

"Keep your language clean, and keep your tone respectful, when you speak to us. This is a very serious matter."

"It's not a *matter* at all, it's just a figment of someone's smutty imagination."

"But wouldn't you agree that, by creating and circulating pornographically suggestive images like this, you are encouraging the smutty imaginations of people like that? And another interesting question would be: was your 'model'" (she nuanced the word rather cleverly) "a boy or a girl?"

"A boy. I think. It's a long time ago."

"He was a very pretty boy, then. Strikingly effeminate! Or perhaps it was a girl after all?"

"No, it was a boy. I'm almost certain of that. But it didn't matter. For this project, it wasn't important."

Once again, Guardian Rebek'a laughed. "Girl or boy—for this guy it makes no difference, he likes it *both* ways!"

"Colleague, that doesn't help!"

"You know I didn't mean it like that. And, yes, I'm pretty sure that it was a boy. I'll remember his name in a moment."

"But this near-naked child could easily be imagined as a girl, couldn't it? As a girl without her bikini top.

Topless. Helpless. *Exposed*."

"Lots of little girls like that leave off their bikini top, or wear plain swimming trunks."

"Thereby exposing their breasts!"

"But she hasn't *got* any breasts!"

He regretted it immediately.

"No, I mean 'he', of course. Look, it *was* a boy, and even if you imagine that somehow it's not a boy but a topless girl, it's still a girl who hasn't got any breasts yet, it's just a child."

"So you're admitting to creating images that could serve as pornography for either homo- *or* heterosexual pedophiles. You're a very talented man, Mr. Burk!"

He noticed that for the first time she had addressed him as "Mister", but ironically rather than respectfully.

"This is nonsense, and you know it."

"The image speaks for itself. But even if it didn't, what does the caption say? Please read it to us."

"It says 'WATER PARADISE: Come and find what you've always dreamed of!'"

"Exactly. *Quod erat demonstrandum*."

Both her colleagues stared at her.

"Or, in other words: I rest my case."

"This is crazy! I didn't write that caption. I just adapted it from the one that we used back on Terra, when I was in my last job. You know who thought it up? It was the director of the municipal recreational center that I told you about."

"A fellow conspirator, in all likelihood. Another pedophile."

"No, an elderly lady, a senior figure in local government. Now a retired Guardian. I can confirm that by transmission link to Terra, and she can explain how the image was made, too. We can find out the boy's full name. We had a contract with him; both his parents signed it. I think his name was Byllie."

"All that is, I'm afraid, only of abstract interest. We have to make a decision now, on the basis of the information that is already available to us. We'll very shortly be going into high slide. The ship's transmission channels are already completely overloaded. We can't compromise the safety of thousands of people to indulge little matters like this."

Guardian Rebek'a, with a leer: "Or, in other words: your goose is cooked, little Burk!"

"No, Colleague, it doesn't mean that at all. Mr. Burk, your despicable crime, assuming that it was committed—and you will notice, please, that we're in no way presuming your guilt—was committed on Terra, and should therefore be investigated, and possibly tried, there where it happened, and where all necessary witnesses can be called to give evidence in person. Evidence against you or in your defense. It would not be appropriate for us to stage a formal prosecution here on the ship, even if we still had the time. You do understand that this is in your own best interests?"

"Yes."

"Nor would it be right to allow you to disembark on Lemnos, whether as a free man or as a fettered prisoner, because the very nature of the accusations leveled against you would place you in constant danger of being lynched by the settlers. As Colleague Rebek'a has already pointed out."

She said this with such conviction that Burk could almost—though not quite—imagine that she really did have his best interests at heart.

"I therefore make the following recommendation, hoping that my Colleagues will concur: that you be held on board this ship, confined to your present quarters, when we dock at the Gate of Lemnos; that you return to Terra with us (after all, you have a fully paid return ticket); and that you there submit to proper investigation of these charges against you. Because you are innocent until proved guilty, and because there will to the best of my knowledge be no children on board on the return journey, you will not be held in close confinement. But for your own protection you will be kept under supervision."

She looked at both her colleagues in turn.

"Are we in agreement?"

They nodded.

"Then we must all sign the transcript, when the clerk has made a clean draft, but, whatever happens, before we go into the transportation pods. Mr. Scribe, please call in the escort to take Mr. Burk back to his quarters. Oh, and put him back on full AdPop rations. Did I say he was a prisoner? He's not really a prisoner, is he?"

CHAPTER SIX
FRAMED

"His quarters", the Goddess had said. This actually turned out to be the uncomfortable holding cell, and not his regular accommodation, but it would only be for a matter of hours, or a day at the most, and then they would all be moved to the pods.

The other passengers were busy packing their things ready for disembarkation. Better now than after coming out of the pods, when most of them would be feeling groggy. Docking was held to be the most tricky and dangerous part of space travel. Many of the passengers would be hysterical, and even the crew would be tense and nervous, especially as the ship would be attempting the docking maneuver at the Gate for the first time.

Burk didn't need to pack. After the *Starstretcher* had left the Gate to start the return journey, he could leave the cell and go back to his original, and much more comfortable, AdPop (Lower Executive Level) quarters on Level E.

One thing was perfectly clear to him. He had been framed, and in the crudest possible way. It couldn't have happened like this back on Terra—the whole misunderstanding would have been cleared up promptly and unbureaucatically. Terra might be a mess, but it was still (theoretically) a democracy, where citizens, at least in the heartland areas of the Anglo Zone, could expect to be governed by the rule of law. Procedures had to be followed. Prosecutors had to have reasons for having you tasered, locked up, interrogated. And you would be dealt with by legal professionals. Only Guardian Sousanna ("from Crime and Security") even remotely fitted that description. If this had happened on Terra, Ex-Guardian Grade III Silvia—that was her name, bless her!—would soon have secured his release, and maybe even won him an official apology (well, maybe not).

But they weren't on Terra. Out in space, things sometimes had to be improvised. Guardian Sousanna was right, though: he would indeed have to go back to Terra to face the charges, since that was where the supposed offence was believed to have taken place.

Nor was there, to Burk's mind, anything wrong with that particular law. The rule had been introduced to discourage criminals from assuming that, if they did a runner out into space and were caught, it would be so difficult to organize a trial at such a distance from Terra that the authorities might even let them off with a warning. Suspects were always sent back. That wasn't the official explanation, though. Officially, it was said that the new rule was there to protect suspected criminals from being given short shrift by kangaroo courts and then lynched by the settlers. (Perhaps that was partially true as well. It would be nice to think so.)

Burk would therefore be dragged back to Terra to be properly investigated, an investigation that would in all likelihood lead to his almost immediate release. He would then be invited to apply for jobs on Terra of the kind that he had had before. There would be no opportunity to fly out to Lemnos again any time in the near future: he couldn't afford the ticket as a passenger, and even if they gave him clearance they probably wouldn't let him take up another job on a people transporter. He wouldn't be able to help Milliya as she had asked him to.

"They." "They" were whoever it was that didn't want him to land on Lemnos. He had been framed, but only to stop him from disembarking at the Gate. Once back on Terra, there would be no need to persecute him further. Why stir up more resentment? Burk might have powerful friends who could cause trouble.

Actually, he didn't. Ex-Guardian Silvia was a sweet old lady who was known for doing good in the community, that was all, and there were no influential former colleagues of hers whom she could pester indignantly with strange tales about a harmless AdPop called Burk who had been set up by sinister forces of evil within the ranks of the Guardians.

Somehow, someone had heard about the promise that he had made to Milliya. Namely, to do what she said she *couldn't* do: to go to Lemnos and find out what was happening there. And that person had presumably betrayed them. Milliya had been forced to change her identity—she would only be safe so long as they believed her to be dead.

She was indeed now on her way to Lemnos, but if, as "Guardian Jo-anna", she was part of the ship's contingent of Security Guardians, she couldn't necessarily expect to be allowed off the ship. The shuttles would be full to bursting with settlers and wealthy honeymooners, so there would be no room for non-paying tourists.

It might even be dangerous for her if she tried to go through a control scanner. What if the real Guardian Jo-anna had had some sort of implant, perhaps an identity chip with her medical notes and her Last Will and Testament, or a security clearance tag from her last job? All of that would show up under the scanner. It would be asking too much to expect them *not* to look at what was there (or *wasn't* there) on the screen in front of them.

So—she still needed Burk for this assignment. He would have to look for the information that she needed. She wouldn't be able to do more than try her best to protect him, and there was no guarantee that she'd be able to do that effectively. Essentially, Burk was on his own. That was the situation as it had been.

Now the situation had changed. The enemy—those "very powerful, very dangerous people" she had referred to—had struck back. Burk had been neutralized. He would not be allowed to land on Lemnos. He would be shipped back to Terra in temporary disgrace, before being absolved of any dreadful pedophile crimes and allowed to take his place in society again as a normal, harmless AdPop. Not for him the thrills of asking awkward questions and perhaps discovering dark and embarrassing secrets.

For Milliya it would be different. She was the initiator of this dangerous matter, and would therefore—if she broke from the cover of her new identity—be hunted down and killed. When they finally cornered her, the tasers would be quietly set to "HIGH", which was not merely painful, it was more than any human being could survive. Burk had seen old recordings of the execution of some of Ciaran Burke's men. The taserings had been so agonizingly painful that, after a public outcry, this form of execution was suspended in favor of more "humane" methods. When they got to Milliya, they would want to make very sure that, later on, there would be no surreptitious calls from hospital, no journalists at her bedside, no statements to the media, no cunning lawyers getting her released on a technicality.

How could Burk now help her, though? He looked about the holding cell, considering what there was available to hand that could conceivably be used as a weapon. When Slabface came in, he could…smother her with his blanket? Throw water in her face? Stab her with his dental hygiene unit, which they had so thoughtfully brought over from his regular accommodation? Choke her with the remains of his AdPop rations, or bludgeon her to death with the lightweight tray? Guardians were trained to maim or kill using such everyday objects, but Burk certainly wasn't, and they hadn't left any tasers or stun-clubs conveniently lying around.

Hand to hand, he would scarcely stand a chance against any of them. Even Ex-Guardian Silvia back on Terra would have remembered enough of her training to be able to hurl him about the room like a puppet. And even if by some miracle he won, where would he go afterwards? The outlook was bleak.

Once Slabface's lifeless body (a pleasing but, it had to be admitted, unlikely image) had been found, they would come looking for him in overwhelming force, and they would make sure to track him down. The *Starstretcher* might be enormous, but there were only so many places where you could hide, and they would know where these were far better than he did. It would only be a matter of time before they found him.

* * * * * * *

BURK WAS DISTURBED IN HIS MUSINGS by the door whirring open. It wasn't someone sent to torment or interrogate him, or even the additional AdPop rations that Guardian Sousanna had promised him, but the little clerk, hunched, and shaking with nervousness.

"Keep your voice low. Better not to speak! It'll be death if they find me here."

He perched himself on the side of the sleeping ledge, leant forward so that his face was close to Burk's—he was sweating heavily—and whispered, "My name is Scribe Jacoob, and I'm your friend. Your only true friend on this ship."

Scribes were the lowest of the low in the ranks of the administration, except for the illiterate cleaners and laborers. They were AdPops with just enough education to take notes, move files and make copies. Above them in the pyramid were all those like the Secretaries and the Administrators who carried responsibility and were involved in decision-making on some level. Scribes were office coolies, less reliable than data processing equipment but more mobile and, if they were women or young men, sometimes more decorative. If Burk had dropped out of college, this would probably have been his fate, too.

"Don't be silly! You're part of this charade to set me up as a child-abuser!"

"Yes. I know."

"Oh." Burk hadn't expected that.

"Do you think I have any choice? I do what I'm ordered to, that's my job. If they want someone to take notes at their *informal hearing*"—he gave the words an ironic emphasis—"notes which, you may remember, would *be solely for their convenience....*"

"The whole thing was a sham! And you know that too."

"Yes, of course."

"Just to stop me from reaching Lemnos. To have me sent home in disgrace, charged with imaginary crimes. And then, back on Terra—"

"No, there would be no 'then'. Your crimes are imaginary, Mr. Burk. The charges will miraculously disappear. There is no transcript. And as for the notepad—if anyone should bother to look, all that they'll find is my shopping list, of souvenirs from Lemnos. My grandchildren expect me to bring them something: some colored Lemnos dust, perhaps; a tiny Goro-nut, if I can afford it; some pretty crystals. Assuming, naturally, that I'm one of the lucky crew-members, and that I get a place on the shuttle to go down to the surface for some sightseeing." He smiled sweetly. "Do you have any family, Mr. Burk?"

"You know very well that I don't! Actually, you seem to know a lot. You probably know what all this is about. Why they won't let me disembark. Any bright suggestions?"

"You tell *me*, Mr. Burk."

Should he risk it? He would risk it!

"*Sqot*. I'm guessing that it's about *sqot*."

"Dear Mr. Burk, why do these conversations always have to take so long? Of course it's about *sqot*. What else could it possibly be about?"

"But I don't know anything about *sqot*. Except that apparently it's interesting. Though I imagine it gets boring after a while—all that green stuff, miles and miles of it."

"You've been asked to find out more about *sqot*, Mr. Burk, and to convey that information to Terra. I know that, so you can assume that there are a lot of other people who know it as well. And not everybody is happy about it. You know how it goes: you stick your nose in where it's not wanted, and you get it chopped off. Sending you back to Terra on a trumped-up charge that disappears magically just as you arrive home—that strikes me as being a very mild response. Suspiciously mild, if I might say."

"You're not really a Scribe, are you?"

"Oh yes, I'm a Scribe. Let's say that I have *certain other commitments*, though, as well as my professional duties."

"So—why don't they kill me then, if I'm so inconvenient? It wouldn't be too difficult to organize."

"Who are these 'they' in your question, Mr. Burk? The Terran Government, whatever your own or my personal opinion of it might be, is publicly committed to the rule of law."

Burk snorted, and the Scribe indicated that he should try not to make any noise. He edged closer to Burk, and spoke very softly.

"Mr. Burk, there are other groups, other forces, who are interested in the flora and fauna of Lemnos. Groups, or forces, who are perhaps *less* committed to the rule of law than is comfortable to think about. More than one of these groups may be represented on this ship. For that matter, please tell me, Mr. Burk: which group do *you* happen to belong to?"

CHAPTER SEVEN
DON'T UNDERESTIMATE PEOPLE

"I DON'T BELONG TO ANY GROUP. I don't even know that we're on the same side. Which group do *you* belong to, then? And what do you want from me?"

"I could tell you that. I could tell you a lot of things. But I don't know if I can trust you. Your behavior has been somewhat *peculiar*, Mr. Burk, and my life is in as much danger as yours. Let me say this much: I know that you have been asked to find out more about *sqot*, but I don't know who it was who gave you this commission. If I knew that, it would throw considerable light on this situation. I would understand more clearly who it is that we are dealing with here on the *Starstretcher*. Perhaps it might save your life. And mine."

"Oh Mr. Scribe, you say that you're my friend, 'my only friend on this ship', but I reckon you're just a spy, doing the dirty work for the Guardians. What's in it for you? Promotion? You want to be a Guardian yourself? You want to be a Lemnos settler? It's the oldest trick in the book: 'Trust me, I'm your friend.' And then I get shafted."

In his agitation, Burk knocked the tray with what

was left of his AdPop rations onto the floor. It didn't make a particularly loud clatter, but the Scribe jumped up nervously.

"Mr. Burk, I've already been here far too long. I mustn't be caught with you. You're foolish not to trust me, but if you're not prepared to do that, then I beg you: don't trust anyone. *Anyone*. Including the person who put you up to this. Test them all. Question them all. Take nothing—and no-one—for granted. And next time, please, I'm not 'Mr. Scribe', I'm Jacoob."

The clatter had indeed been heard. Slabface stood in the now open doorway, her taser pointed at Burk. But it was Jacoob, flustered and confused, who reacted like the boy caught with his hand in the cookie jar.

"Guardian…?"

"Abi. You have no authorization to be with the prisoner!"

Jacoob winced, and adopted a servile manner.

"Guardian Abi, I'm sorry that you were not informed."

As if low-grades had to be briefed on everything! But it did no harm to flatter them.

"He's no longer a prisoner, he's just under supervision now."

"So what are you doing here?"

"He complained about his rations, and I came to find out what the problem was. He's been put back on full AdPop rations, did you know that?"

"We were told that."

She pointed to the rations now lying scattered on the

floor.

"That stuff's dirty now. You can put it all in the waste bin and I'll bring the prisoner, sorry, the *supervisee* a new set of rations. But you should go now, or we'll all be in trouble."

As Jacoob busied himself with clearing up the debris of the rations, Burk thought how much better Slabface's command of English was than her boss Cruella's! Despite her unprepossessing appearance—to be honest, she was downright ugly—she was not out of the running for Grade II promotion. Burk made a mental note not to underestimate people so quickly in future.

"Abi" was probably short for "Abyssinia" rather than "Abigail"—there had been a craze for names of countries that no longer existed, like "Mali" or "Gambia".

"Come on, hurry up, there's someone else, someone important, coming to see him in a moment."

"Oh, sorry."

Jacoob's servile hunch at once became even more pronounced.

"I hope you won't mention that I was here? There's no reason for anyone to know, is there? Everyone's so touchy at the moment."

"Yeah, and you know why? It's because we're going into the pods soon. No, I won't say anything. But you owe me one, right? And don't forget that."

"Thank you so much! You're so kind! And, no, I won't forget, I promise you!"

Guardian Abi had put the fear into him. What would

she demand from Jacoob as the price of her silence? Probably sex. There was a lot of corrupt exploitation like that going on, however much contacts between the strata might be discouraged officially, and it wasn't likely that Slabface had any male Guardians battering their way to her door. Not that Jacoob was much to look at, either.

After they had both gone out, Slabface locking the door behind her—so much for him being a supervisee rather than a prisoner!—Burk considered his position. Had he been right not to trust Jacoob? If he had told him about Milliya, he might have been putting her life in danger.

As for the "different groups", he had observed differences between the three senior Guardians, to be sure, but who wanted what exactly? The plan to set him up was clear, but did they all support it or was one of them perhaps out of step with the others, with a different agenda, and biding their time?

Sqot was what it was all about. Milliya had told him that the green stuff was being cleared on a grand scale, even though it hadn't been properly studied yet. It wasn't as though there were many life-forms that had been discovered in the course of the Terran exploration of the universe so far, and here was one of them already almost on the verge of extinction! Milliya wanted him to find out more, and get the information back to Terra.

She had given him a contact name. Burk was good with information: he knew all the tricks for circumventing the censors, getting round transmission problems, disseminating what needed to be spread. The authorities on the other hand were slow, and it was fun to embarrass them. It was what had attracted him to his profession in the first place. It was also what had prevented him from having a successful career and even landed him in detention a couple of times.

Someone important was apparently now on their way to see him, presumably one of the three Guardians. Maybe one of them was about to break ranks? Which would it be?

The door opened. It was Guardian Adriyan.

* * * * * * *

IF LOOKS COULD KILL, the look that Burk gave Guardian Adriyan would have rated as grievous bodily harm at the very least.

"Look what the cat has brought in! Something tells me I'm not surprised to see you."

"Now that's not a very friendly way to greet someone who has only your best interests at heart. I ought to go into a big, sulky huff, being treated like that. Talk about showing a girl a good time! It's just as well that my social life is going so well. And I came with such high expectations…"

"Oh, shut up! We all know what this is about: I get screwed—"

"*Language*, sweetheart!"

"—to stop me asking awkward questions about what you've been doing on Lemnos. Eradicating species, or something of that kind?"

As the Scribe had said, "a lot of other people" knew what Burk was up to, and so he could assume that Guardian Adriyan was one of them.

"Believe me, that's nothing to do with me. And it's not what the Government has been doing, either."

"I'm not inclined to believe one single word you say."

"Then perhaps I should make myself clearer. It isn't the Government that's destroying *sqot*, it's the settlers, and we don't know why. Someone is encouraging them to do it, and we'd like to know who that is."

"And why should I believe you?"

"Well, for starters: my mother always said that I had an honest face."

"Look, you're going to send me back to Terra, to cover all this up. Even if I don't end up in gaol, who's ever going to give me a job again? Just leave me alone!"

"I wish I could, Mr. Burk" (all of a sudden the temperature in the room seemed to drop) "but you're in deepest you-know-what, much deeper than you realize. What do you actually know about *sqot*?"

"I know that it's a life-form, a kind of elaborate moss, that it's only found on Lemnos, and that we're rapidly exterminating it."

"That's all?"

"That's enough, surely? That we're destroying one of the few known forms of life in the universe…."

"No, I meant: is that all you know about *sqot*?"

"Well, yes."

"Then let me help you out. But we can start with the exterminating, if you like."

"You should be ashamed. The whole human race should be ashamed."

"When Lemnos was first discovered, three-quarters of its surface area was covered by *sqot*. Given that there are other forms of life on Lemnos, admittedly not very advanced ones—"

"Goro-nuts!"

"Yes, among others. I think you get my point. As I said: three-quarters of Lemnos covered by *sqot*. That suggests a highly successful species, well adapted to its natural environment. It also contributes to the great natural beauty of the planet, especially when seen from the Gate of Lemnos."

"At least I'll get to see that, I hope, before you ship me back to Terra. So that I have something to tell my kids and grandkids—when I finally get down to continuing the noble family line."

"I'm sure that a viewing can be arranged, but I fear you're going to be disappointed."

"Why?"

"Because there is no Green Planet any more. Most of the *sqot* has gone."

"I thought so! And this is the crime that you want to keep hidden from the Terran public!"

But Guardian Adriyan was now listening not to Burk but to some inner voice—

"Yes, most of the *sqot* has gone. The settlers burned it, to clear the land. They tore it up and used it by the ton as fuel for their ovens and generators. They have tried to reduce it chemically, to make paint and dyes, though with little success. Some of the settlers eat it, cooked or raw, but not everyone is willing to do so, because of the way the *sqot* moves, the way it *pulsates*, as they say, in your hands—"

"Ah, sweet Adriyan, I knew I'd find you here!"

Guardian Rebek'a was already in the room. Neither Adriyan, obsessed by his reverie, nor Burk, appalled by what he was hearing, had noticed her enter.

"Don't you think you've told him enough, Colleague? I mean, when all that gets back to Terra, our precious Government is not going to look very good, is it?"

Burk was still reeling.

"You've doctored all the images, haven't you? Nobody was to know. The crews, the settlers: did you buy people's silence, or use threats? How long can you hide such an atrocity?"

"Dear, dear boy, you don't know the half of it! Although it's right under your nose. I had great hopes for you. For a brief moment, I even thought we might be an item, you and I. You're going back to Terra, but you won't be talking to anyone except us—at least, not until we've found out the truth. There are several matters that you can help us with."

He turned to his colleague.

"Better that he should be in close confinement, I think."

"No. Better that he should be *free.*"

Guardian Adriyan gawped at her, amazed at what she was saying.

"Yes, Adriyan dear, we've come to the parting of the

ways. Burk: we are going. We'll soon be climbing into the pods, and there are things to arrange first."

"Are you out of your mind? Burk: step back! You're staying here!"

Adriyan held out a taser, but not the way a professional would; he looked more like a child with his first paintbrush. Rebek'a kicked it out of his hand. Burk had never seen anyone so big move so fast. Briefly, they circled each other. Adriyan didn't stand a chance. He was Martial Arts, First Year Guardian training; she was a big cat that hadn't fed for a week.

She soon had him in a fearsome grip, and Burk waited for the sound of his neck snapping. But it never came. Instead, she pressed a spot on his neck and he sagged together, unconscious.

"Give me the taser, little boy."

Burk hesitated. She looked at him, but didn't get up.

"Come on, give me the taser. We need to get out of here."

Burk handed her the taser. She made a few adjustments to the controls, got to her feet and, standing over Adriyan, fired a death-shot straight into him. He spasmed and grunted as it hit him, pulled painfully back into consciousness for a few dying moments, before slumping like a dead-weight against the floor. Smoke rose from his body. Burk was horrified.

"Why did you do that?"

She was already wiping the taser clean. She slipped the gun into Guardian Adriyan's hand and arranged his fingers around it. It looked to Burk almost as if she had done this before.

"Not foolproof, I know, but there won't be any elaborate forensics. It was suicide! His pretty boyfriend had given him the push—Dhavid will be very cooperative, I'm sure, the arrangements have been made—so he came here looking for you, unlocking the door and promising you freedom, in return for…love? But you laughed at him and ran off. His personal life was in ruins, and now he'd screwed up his career. So he took the coward's way out."

Burk stared at the body.

"Did you have to do that? He was already unconscious."

"Welcome to the world of the grownups! But don't waste any time over *him*. Nobody will miss him: he was a pathetic creature, a pervert, and he didn't do his job properly. You won't say anything, though, not if you value your life."

"But it was an execution."

"Let's concentrate on *you* now, Burk. You have things to tell the world, don't you? That suits me fine! While I clear up here a little, you will go quietly and unobtrusively to Level F. Room 106. That'll be easy enough. The door is open. Go in and wait for me there. Don't touch anything. If somebody challenges you, you have been released on parole under my supervision, and I am on my way. If you stay calm, there is only one person on this ship who can cause serious trouble, and that particular lady is busy at this moment. You won't be in that room for very long, I promise you.

The pods are already being activated."

"Why are doing this? You work for the Government. You have a career. So?"

"Ah, little Burk! You're a sweet boy. I wish I had some time to play with you myself. Not everything is about selfishness, surely? Sometimes you need to see the *bigger picture*. But Adriyan here—poor deceased Adriyan, may he rest in peace—was right about one thing: you don't know the half of it! But that doesn't matter. You'll know enough, when we've briefed you, to say what you need to say. And that will give you a place in the history of the universe!

Now—get moving."

CHAPTER EIGHT
THE *STARSTRETCHER*

SHE WAS RIGHT, IT WAS EASY to find Level F, Room 106. Burk knew the *Starstretcher* well enough. He hadn't been on Level A, the command level, very often, and there was a Level 0 that was completely off bounds, full of military and scientific gadgets. Level B, where he'd been confined, was the lower administration level, and Level C, where he worked, had offices and recreational facilities. Below that were the living units, starting with the Guardians' quarters (D), then the AdPop crew members (E), and from F downwards the ship's passengers.

The massive thrust units for the Starstretcher's slide propulsion were on the outside of the ship, but inside were the generators and a whole level containing these and other technical and maintainence equipment. Finally, there were levels devoted to food stores and water creation and storage, and a limited amount of high-value freight. (The *Starstretcher* doubled as a priority freighter, but with its high slide transportation pods it was too expensive for transporting ordinary freight items.) This was also where the punishment cells were.

The levels that Burk knew best were C, where he worked in the Social and Recreational Department, and E, where he slept; also B, because of the constant need for him to liaise with Guardian officials. He'd only been to Level F once before, to interview an apparently newsworthy passenger, the wife of a wealthy settler who'd been on a shopping excursion to Terra (an almost unheard-of luxury). Holding the interview in her suite had been her idea. Burk should have guessed what was expected to happen—what he was expected to do—but he had been curious to see how the privileged were housed on the transporter, and he was so obsessionally preoccupied with thoughts of Milliya that he didn't visualize the attack until it happened.

When she opened the door to him, Burk found that, though she was old enough to be his mother, she wasn't suitably dressed for that role. Indeed, the word "dressed" was rather a misnomer on this occasion. He accepted a generous shot of highly intoxicating Lemnian Goro-whiskey, from a large flask that was already almost empty (and would have cost him a month's salary, had Burk ever been into that particular tipple); tried to avoid staring at the voluptuous, undulating charms that were only inches away from him, and moving ominously closer all the time; and began the interview.

Gloriya had once been a movie starlet, specializing (surprise, surprise!) in minor glamor roles, in the good old days of the film business before actors were almost completely replaced by androids. (Androids didn't oversleep, throw hissy fits, forget their lines or demand excessive fees, and if they *did* occasionally make a mistake they could easily be reprogrammed.) Today, only a small number of roles in movies were played by humans—and even then you couldn't always be completely sure....

She had married a businessman who was one of the second generation of Lemnos settlers: not the pioneers who had tamed the planet, but the developers and land speculators who had raped it. Bored out of her mind by her elderly husband and the lack of shopping opportunities on Lemnos, she had thrown herself into charity work, assisting noisily in a project to insert orphaned children from the slums of Terra into childless marriages on Lemnos. (The fact that these marriages were usually loveless as well as childless, with pleasure androids filling the emotional void, was of no concern to her.) This conveniently allowed her to commute to and from the planet on a regular basis— and keep her wardrobe nicely restocked. She was now returning from such a trip to Terra; and far below her luxury suite was a more functionally furnished dormitory accommodating the latest batch of lucky orphans that she was escorting to new lives in the Zora System.

This much Burk, sitting beside her on her sofa, had already been able to ascertain and record for the feature about her that he was planning, for the series *Onboard Personalities*, before the fatal wardrobe malfunction occurred. One of Gloriya's very ample (though surgically modified) charms, held in place rather than contained by what was undoubtedly a prohibitively expensive mechanical uplift system, burst from its moorings. The *Starstretcher*'s artificially-maintained gravity pulled the delightful object downwards, and its owner with it, straight onto Burk's lap. Drinks were scattered, Gloriya murmured huskily, "Oh my darling", and lunged for him, and Burk fled for his life.

He had then spent an eternity going round in circles on Level F, looking for a means of escape—by lift or staircase—that *didn't* take him past Room 004, where the love-hungry lady might still be lurking in wait for him. Unfortunately, most of the means of transportation between F and the other levels were situated so as to be convenient for the occupants of the luxury suites, so it took a while before Burk found a back staircase used mostly by waiters and cleaners, by which time he was reasonably familiar with the layout of Level F.

Room 106 was not a luxury suite. It was nowhere near 004. And Gloriya would in the meantime have moved on to other quarry and likely forgotten even what Burk looked like. (He may not have been able to meet her more urgent needs, but at least her honor had been satisfied by means of an article in *Onboard Personalities*, illustrated with a flattering image from the passenger database, about her noble and self-sacrificing work for the destitute children of Caracas and Greater Dhaka.)

He found the room quickly. There were no incidents on the way, except for an unexpected meeting with

Guardian Abi, whose slab-like physiognomy cracked unexpectedly into a very asymmetrical smile when she saw him. "Hallo supervisee", she said, but walked on past him.

106 was a simple living unit, even smaller than his own, but with no signs that anyone had been using it throughout the whole flight. There were empty rations containers in the kitchen, an old text-reader (that didn't work properly), soiled sheets on the bed and a hetero-geneous collection of cheap cleansers and cosmetics in the bathroom. It had been used *ad hoc*, as temporary housing, maybe for illicit assignations. A love-nest? Only Guardians would be able to organize such a facility on a people transporter. Is this where Slabface would bring Scribe Jacoob for hours of passion? The twilight world of Guardian sex.... It would be a fascinating but very dangerous topic for an article, he thought.

He had barely had time to make himself comfortable when the buzzer rang.

CHAPTER NINE
INTO THE PODS

IT WAS NOT GUARDIAN REBEK'A, he discovered upon opening the door, but Milliya. She pushed forward eagerly, he stepped back in surprise, and so she literally fell into the room on top of him. In this undignified way they found themselves, with neither amatory intention nor time-wasting preliminaries, in a position that was congenial to both of them. There is no need to describe what happened next. The furnishings of the living unit were cheap and badly-designed, not really suitable for "living" in any true sense of the word, even by the reduced standards of Terran society; the fabrics were crumpled and dirty; the color scheme of the unit unappealing. But Burk and Milliya were aware only of each other, and so once again the unit served its purpose well enough.

In-between, Burk needed to get up for a moment to secure the door.

Afterwards, they drank coffee—Milliya had brought some rations packages with her—and Burk asked her for an explanation. How did she know that he would be in F 106?

"Because there is someone who is helping me, a person who is clever and resourceful."

"Guardian Rebek'a?"

"Yes. It's a great honor to have someone so awe-inspiring looking after you. She's so unbelievably talented, there's no limit to what she can achieve. And all this time she's been looking after you as well. She sat in on that stupid 'hearing', although she hates the other Guardians, just so as to keep an eye on you. She has to pretend to be like them, though really she's an idealist."

Burk was puzzled.

"So you don't know?"

He told her about the scene with Guardian Adriyan, and how he had been more or less executed by the "idealist".

Milliya hesitated for barely a second.

"No, she is an idealist. If she feels strongly about something, she'll fight for it with any means that she has. She'll kill, if she needs to—out of *love*."

"But it was terribly cruel, the way she killed him."

"He was one of those creatures of the Government. You know a lot more about *sqot* now, don't you? You know what those scum are doing. He deserved to die."

"She called him a pervert."

This time Milliya looked genuinely surprised.

"Oh. That's weird. That's not like her at all. No, really."

Burk took advantage of her momentary confusion.

"Don't you think there's something strange about

her, something almost monstrous? I'm terrified of her! She could break my back without even working up a sweat."

"Well, darling, so could I!" Milliya laughed. "You know, you're a terrible old drone. Leave the fighting to us Guardian Girls!"

"Something…a bit unnatural even?"

"Don't talk like that."

Milliya was now coldly serious.

"She is a great woman. Great people *are* strange. They're not like us. We may not always understand them, but we can follow them, admire what they're doing, and try to be like them. For you, it's also hard that you're a man. Thousands of years ago, women like Colleague Rebek'a were burned at the stake as witches—by men. Today, they rule the universe."

Milliya told him to get ready for the pods. It wasn't necessary to wash or brush your teeth—you would effectively be "frozen" in the pod—but most people still did so out of habit. He had nothing to pack. His gear was mostly back in his quarters on Level E, where he wasn't sure how they'd react if he turned up without a "supervisor"; and, far worse, if he had someone pack it for him, it would be a clear sign that he was not intending to be staying on board for the return journey, as they probably still assumed.

"I expect that Colleague Rebek'a has put them off the scent by saying that she is supervising you. With luck, no-one will notice you're gone until you're already on Lemnos."

"Won't anyone come looking for me?"

"Let's just hope they don't. Who'll have the time? You're not *that* important! Everyone's going to be very busy, very stressed out. People will be going into the pods. And this is the first time that the *Starstretcher* will be docking at the Gate. Anyway: who would it be, coming looking for you? Colleague Adriyan is dead. Colleague Sousanna—she's the real danger!—will be disembarking, too. She's got a secret commission to fulfill on Lemnos (but don't tell anyone, it's highly confidential). Colleague Rebek'a will be returning to Terra."

"How are you going to get me onto the shuttle?"

"*Both* of us, my dear! I've made all the necessary adjustments, and nothing awkward will show up on the scanner. It was surprisingly easy. It was actually harder for *me* than for you, because they don't like giving Guardians tourist leave on Lemnos. It fills up the shuttles too quickly, so only a handful of senior Guardians usually get to go down to the surface. I had to think of a duty that would require me to do that. Clever girl, eh?"

"But why did you risk this? It would have been much easier for Guardian Rebek'a...."

"You dimwit! I see that I'm going to continue having to do the thinking for both of us. What happens if they discover that Rebek'a made the changes? She'd be a sitting duck, trapped on the *Starstretcher* on its way back to Terra. But if they find out that someone called 'Guardian Jo-anna', who doesn't exist, made them, and you and I are already on Lemnos, where there'll be plenty of places to hide...? *Capisce?*"

Yes, he understood. They had planned it well. He also noticed, in passing, that she had referred to "Rebek'a", and not "Colleague Rebek'a", an unusual, even insolent, level of informality between Guardians so different in rank.

* * * * * *

THEY SLEPT FOR A SHORT WHILE, more for the intimacy than because they were tired.

The moment that they stepped out of the door, it was apparent that something was happening. People were rushing about, calling out to each other, in strangely high-pitched voices, urgent reminders or vital pieces of information, embracing, waving, and panicking because of what they had forgotten, or maybe forgotten that they had forgotten. No-one had luggage with them, because there would be time between coming out of the pods and having to be at the disembarkation points: time to assemble the group or the family, have breakfast, and collect the cases. But the packing was already done—or was now being done at the last minute—because the passengers had all been told not to pack just before arrival. Coming out of the pods, they would be cold and disoriented; a few would be seriously depressed or anxious; and some would have muscular aches and pains. It wouldn't be good, in this miserable condition, to have to pack their luggage as well.

Word had got around among the passengers that this was a virgin voyage to Lemnos for the *Starstretcher*, and that many of the crew were nervous about the docking procedure. The ship was new and almost "state of the art", but it was very big, and the technology on the control vessel was from a different generation. What if the automatic mode didn't work, and the Commander had to do the docking maneuver himself from the bridge, synchronizing each delicate step with the captain of the control vessel? Good that the Commander was known to be one of the very best pilots in the Fleet! There was so much to worry about, so much that could go wrong!

Burk and Milliya were with some likelihood the only "passengers" who *weren't* worrying, who were in fact even hoping for some extra confusion and last-minute technical problems, so as to make the procedures at the Gate as chaotic and inefficient as possible.

What was always absolutely essential was to get the pod-numbers right, since the containers needed to be programmed differently for small children, the elderly, and those with certain medical conditions; also for second- or third-time travelers, because the body tended to adapt itself slightly to the "freezing" mechanism, necessitating different values to be coded in when the unit was programmed.

Milliya's pod was on a different tier to Burk's. The Guardians were always placed together—on the principle that, if there happened to be a riot (of cold, miserable passengers, thought Burk, demanding their money back?), the forces of law and order would then be well-positioned to deal with it. The Guardians' pods were larger and more comfortable than the standard ones, which was pointless, as pointless as the "luxury containers" offered to wealthy passengers (like Gloriya, no doubt), because once inside a pod you'd go out almost like a light when it was activated, and when you came to, some light-years further down the road, the pod wasn't the kind of place that you'd want to loll about in, enjoying your cooked breakfast.

Burk found that one of his neighbors was going to be handsome crewman Dhavid, who was wearing a sleek black training suit and natty black slippers. (Sports gear was standard wear for the transportation pods, which were very cold at the end of the high slide run and often not as clean as they should be.) Burk didn't want to be so tasteless as to ask him whether his outfit was intended to be a fashion statement or whether he was already in mourning for his deceased friend, but Dhavid spoke up straightaway, and with unexpected emotion.

Your actions could come back to haunt you, he wailed. If he had known that Guardian Adriyan— such a kind and considerate man!—would ever do something so foolish, he would never have ended their relationship, never, never. There must have been some other reason.

Of course, the age difference had made their staying together impossible. As a young man, he had *social needs* that his partner simply couldn't meet. He was too old for Dhavid, too sedate, there were hip, fun things—he was sure that Burk knew exactly what sort of things he was talking about; Burk quickly professed not to!—*activities* that Guardians would not be allowed to participate in. Contrary to all his expectations, he burbled, the *Starstretcher* had had a lively "scene" on this voyage, but you couldn't keep on turning up with some elderly Guardian on your arm, not if you valued your reputation. Nevertheless, he had cried his eyes out when he heard the news. He would treasure his intimate memories of Guardian Adriyan—and "we shall not see his like again"—yet honor him by *moving on*, because it was in moving on to new horizons, to new friendships, that the true meaning of life lay, did it not? *Etc., etc.*

It was a huge relief for Burk when the signal finally came for them to climb into the pods and lock the containers from the inside. He made a couple of small adjustments on the control panel (the music that he would like to hear when the pod was deactivated, for example). Within a few minutes, he and several thousand passengers, staff and crew were unconscious and moving into the "freeze" stage.

On the whole ship, only the members of the skeleton crew, a tiny group of hardy warriors strapped into unbelievably expensive survival suits, were still conscious. They had all passed a rigorous selection procedure and been trained to withstand the immense forces to which the human body is subjected in interstellar high slide. Only they had the privilege of witnessing the astounding distance of space that the *Starstretcher* was now crossing, albeit in a throbbing, incomprehensible blur of light.

CHAPTER TEN
CHOICES GREAT AND SMALL

BURK HAD CHOSEN LOUD AND CHEERFUL MUSIC. If the pod had been a bed, he could perhaps have leaped from it or fallen out of it, whatever was appropriate, but the container didn't offer these options. Nothing at all could be done before the little red light went off, after which he could press a touchscreen button to release the catch on the door, swing the door open, and, chilled to the bone, climb numbly out of his pod. Around him were other half-dead figures, staggering, twitching and stretching. At this precise moment, *Homo sapiens*, conqueror of the universe, was not an attractive sight. Burk made a special point of not looking at Dhavid.

An information screen at the end of the tier indicated the date, ship's time, artificial temperature and humidity, the name of the ship, the flight number, and (of most urgent importance) the estimated time left until docking at the Gate of Lemnos. The groans coming from some people ("Not enough time!") sent a clear message that this did not suit everyone. Not everyone had packed properly before climbing into the pods.

Also at the end of the tier was a broad stairwell linking it with the other tiers. By the time that Burk had found his way to this, it was already crowded with zombie-like figures lurching up or down the stairs. These were not, for the most part, people looking for lost family members—families were normally given pods in a row on the same tier—but wealthy passengers trying to find their servants (or *vice versa*), crew members on the way to their work-stations, the hungry in search of a quick breakfast snack in one of the ship's many canteens, or simply disoriented individuals who were still trying to wake up properly.

Burk soon found Milliya, who was looking (under the circumstances) surprisingly radiant, and they made their way back to F 106. It had been agreed that this would be a safe place for Burk to wait until just before his illicit disembarkation—it had been arranged with precisely this purpose in mind—and Milliya could wait there with him: since she had been given an assignment on the planet, her first working shift wouldn't begin until she was on the shuttle. There was even a little case for Burk, with living essentials. Someone had kindly slipped into his accommodation unit, packed the items for him, and brought them to F 106.

"It would look peculiar if you disembarked without any luggage! You're not a settler, obviously, but for an AdPop technician, off on a short tour of duty, one small suitcase should be enough. Bachelors travel light!"

"What do you mean: technician?"

"You can't go through the procedures under your

real identity, can you? I've changed what I could in the system, so that you can slip through the controls at the Gate, but I'm not the only person on this ship who can access it. What if some of the data on the *real* you hasn't been deleted? It could be some silly old canteen bill, or an old login, or something like that. Now imagine that that stuff shows up on the scanner, but the information doesn't match with the person that the scanner says you are. That would be bad news, darling, believe me."

"So I'm a different person now?"

"No. I haven't changed the fundamental data on your identity chip—you're still stupid old John Burk, thirty years old, for what he's worth."

She touched his arm affectionately.

"But then—"

"No, I didn't need to do it. What I've done is given you a proxy identity that for about a week will click in every time your chip is accessed. It'll override the data on your chip with the new information that we've programmed."

"And that'll work?"

Burk was highly skeptical, remembering how many times he'd seen the system misfire or partially crash, inevitably when it was something important that you were doing.

"We've tested it. We did a security sweep of the pods on the tier."

"We? But you were frozen, too. And Guardian Rebek'a as well, wasn't she?"

"Rebek'a and I are not the only people involved in

this business."

(Again, the simple "Rebek'a", he noticed.)

"But you couldn't program the scanners on the control vessel, surely?"

"Technically, it could actually be done. But it would be risky. If we transmitted it, someone *unwanted* might pick up the signal, and the data."

"But you could encode it on a higher security level. They wouldn't have time to do a decoding."

"Theoretically, yes. But if we encoded it like that it would really make it look suspicious. Not many messages are transmitted on that sort of security level. So they'd want to know the contents at once. They'd *find* the time. But it wasn't necessary. When we dock with the control vessel, there'll be a massive transfer of data between the ships. They need to know the most boring stuff about the new settlers, for example. But they're not going to clog up the transmission channels with non-vital information, not if they can help it, so—"

"—it'll go through the wire!"

"Ten out of ten for the clever little boy in the front row! When that plug goes into the socket (it's not state of the art technology on Lemnos) our little John Burk smokescreen program will be fed into their system and—hidden among all the settler crap—no one will bother to check it!"

"So—who am I, then?"

Milliya handed him a small identity card.

"This is what will show up on their scanners. I

hope!"

"Markko Mann. Thirty years old. Media technician."

He paused.

"'Media technician'—is this a good idea?"

"Yes?"

"What if they ask me something about my work, ask me to fix something even?"

Milliya laughed.

"This is only to get you on and off the shuttle. Once we're on Lemnos, it'll be a different situation, but there'll be people to help us. Contacts. Help *you*, I should say. You're going underground, but I'm going to be a working girl, 'Guardian Jo-anna', remember?"

"And I don't have any equipment with me. A bit unusual for a technician, surely?"

"No, we thought this through. Markko Mann is a professional image technician, a specialist in doctoring images."

She laughed.

"Just like my dear friend John Burk, the renowned pedophile journalist and image faker!"

"Let's not make jokes about that. I don't think it's particularly funny...."

"Yes, but it has a certain irony, don't you think? And when all this is over, and they're writing the story, and you're the most famous AdPop in the universe, then people *will* laugh. But, seriously, you're good enough at image manipulation to pass as a media technician, aren't you? At least superficially? Who's going to blow your cover?"

"Oh, I can think of all kinds of possibilities! Starting with a proper media technician, you know, the real thing? Some guy with *qualifications*, a framed certificate on the wall…."

"No. There isn't a proper expert on Lemnos. That's the beauty of it! They genuinely need someone, which is why this particular identity is such a good idea. And you don't need equipment, darling, because all the stuff you need—in reality, *won't* need, not where *you're* going—it's there on the planet already, though it's not being used."

"You've organized this well."

"Not me alone. I told you: she's a great woman! But the technology can still let us down. It's going to be dangerous. Still," (with that wonderful smile that Burk loved so much) "where would we be without a bit of danger in our lives? We wouldn't know we were living!"

Burk didn't respond. Milliya noticed that there was something troubling him—she had been top of her year-group in the Guardian exams in Empathy and Social Interaction, among other subjects, so much so that one of her examiners had commented to the others that she was "almost too nice for the job", and that it might one day actually prove to be her undoing. She took his hand.

"I'll have to leave in a moment. I won't see you on the shuttle, or on Lemnos. Someone else will be there to meet 'Markko Mann'. I'll contact you as soon as

I can, though, once I know we're not being watched. It'll be hard for both of us. Remember: I've got a false identity too. 'Guardian Jo-anna.' It's a real pain, being her: she's got an awful profile! If anyone asks me, I'll have to tell them about my exciting hobby—embroidery. And I'm apparently a signed-up member of some wacky female supremacist group that wants all men under sixty to be triaged (which conveniently spares the Emperor): "Sisters, who needs men? We have synthetic sperm!" At least you can re-invent yourself as 'Markko Mann', you could make him an Anti-John Burk, you know, all the things that you've ever wanted to be?"

It worried her that he didn't react.

"I'm sorry—I'm just burbling."

Pause.

"Are you frightened?"

"No, not really."

It sounded unconvincing.

"But there is something?"

"Well, yes—but I'm not sure how to ask you about this. I don't know whether there aren't things that you haven't told me. But it can't be because of your Guardian oath, can it? Because what you're doing, what *we're* doing, is working against the Government. It's subversive."

"Yes, that's true."

"It's a serious matter to break your oath—"

"I know that."

"—but it's more important that you follow your

conscience. There's an enormous crime going on on Lemnos, a crime which is being covered up and which we are going to help to expose. At great personal risk to ourselves. We're going to be the biggest whistle-blowers in the history of the universe."

"Yes."

"Let me get this right: 'Markko Mann' will be met off the shuttle, and taken to a safe hiding place in one of the settler communities, where he will collect evidence, in the form of interviews, leaked documents, images, of the massive destruction of *sqot* by the authorities on Lemnos."

"Yes."

Milliya still didn't get the point.

"What is it that you're trying to say, darling?"

"I've heard that it's the settlers who're destroying the *sqot*, not the Government."

"Of course it's the settlers!"

Milliya now seemed relieved.

"They're the people who live on Lemnos. They're the ones who actually do it, who both carry out and benefit from this disgusting Government policy."

"No, that's not what I meant. I meant that it was the *settlers, and not the Government*. That the settlers were doing it against the wishes of the Government. Initially, even doing it without their knowledge."

Milliya jumped to her feet. She was now highly agitated.

"This is nonsense! Who told you such rubbish? You've been framed, set up, by the Government.

Remember? They've labeled you a pedophile! They don't want you on Lemnos. They don't want you collecting information. And they don't want anyone back on Terra to know about their wickedness."

"I agree. They don't want this to be widely known. They would look really bad, wouldn't they? It would embarrass them. But just because these crimes happened on their watch doesn't make them guilty of committing them."

"Who told you all this?"

"Guardian Adriyan—before he died."

Milliya sat down again.

"Ah, well, there you go! What would you expect him to say? He was a Government man, just like Colleague Sousanna also represents the Terran Government."

"But if, just if, what he said is true, you'd be putting me in the hands of the criminals, those people whose actions we're trying to expose in public. What would that make you? Would you be part of a plot to kill me? Then why did you get me out here on the *Starstretcher* in the first place? I'm here because of you."

"You're wrong, Burk. I would never harm you. But I don't know how to answer your questions."

"Alright, second variant—if what Guardian Adriyan told me is true, yet you don't know what is going on, then are *you* being set up as well?"

He looked at her, but Milliya remained silent.

"And the third variant is—he's wrong. But why should he lie? They were going to send me back to Terra, in disgrace. They knew that I couldn't cause them any real trouble: I had no real proof of anything—not yet, at least. But Guardian Adriyan said that they wanted to speak to me, to 'find out the truth'. What 'truth' could he have been talking about, if not who it was who was really responsible for destroying the *sqot*? And why did he tell me all this, then?"

"I don't know, darling. But there is someone who can answer your questions, if I can reach her before we dock."

Milliya keyed a number into her personal communicator. A few moments later she was whispering into the handpiece, speaking to Guardian Rebek'a. As she did so, the great ship began to judder. The *Starstretcher* had finally reached the Gate of Lemnos. Docking was imminent.

* * * * * * *

IN ORDER TO DOCK, it was necessary for the transporter to slow right down to T-speed. This had been done very smoothly, with only the mildest, almost imperceptible vibration, which Burk and Milliya, completely immersed in their conversation, had hardly noticed at all. Maneuvering the *Starstretcher* into docking position with the control vessel of the Planetary Governorate, the "mother ship" for the shuttles, was, on the other hand, a much more complicated matter.

For all his well-known skill as a pilot, the Commander had not managed to achieve this without subjecting his ship to huge physical forces that had made the *Starstretcher* shake violently. Food fell off the tables in the canteens, people crashed against bulk-heads, many (including Gloriya) screamed in panic, and children became hysterical. Some of the crew even exchanged looks, as if to say: "Does he know what he's doing?"

Yet on the command bridge on Level A, no-one was seriously alarmed. The Commander *did* know what he was doing, and the whole maneuver was carried out, not in automatic mode, but in close contact with the captain of the control vessel, whom the Commander happened to know from years back when they had both been raw recruits at the training academy. In-between the exchange of more sensitive data and control information, they had swapped updates on their marriages and children and agreed to meet for a Goro-whiskey (or even two) while the passengers were being disembarked.

The problem which had caused this slightly bumpy ride was that the *Starstretcher* was too big for the setup at the Gate. The ship's system was programmed to handle this, and virtually any other conceivable eventuality; the Lemnian technology, on the other hand, *wasn't*. Theoretically, it could have been reprogrammed by interstellar transmission; but the sheer quantity of data that would've had to have been pumped through the communication channels would have invited minor transmission errors or black-outs, leading to potentially catastrophic faults in the program.

Better not to risk it. Once the ship had docked, all this data could be comfortably transferred the old-fashioned way, "through the socket", along with great masses of material about the would-be settlers and other disembarkees (including a not completely unimportant little piece of false information about a certain "Markko Mann", who was soon to leave the ship).

Many of the passengers (including Gloriya) were now gawping through portholes in the hope of seeing the fabulous, much lauded spacescape of Lemnos. Unfortunately, the so-called "panoramic portholes" that were a distinctive feature of unit F 004 faced the wrong way, not allowing the occupant a proper view of *anything* of interest, whether Zora, its planets or their moons. If Gloriya had been only slightly less drunk, she might have considered demanding some of her money back (after all, the "space show" had been one of the highlighted attractions of her expensive on-board accommodation).

Other passengers, who happened to have more advantageously positioned portholes, were admiring the view, though some of them at least were also asking themselves or each other why Lemnos was predominantly gray-brown, rather than green. They had come a long, long way, and this was not what they had been led to expect. Could it perhaps be something seasonal, or possibly a freak light-effect?

This little disappointment notwithstanding, there were other interesting phenomena to be seen. For those whose portholes were angled so as to allow them a view of parts of the outer fuselage of the ship, there was the spectacle of the *Starstretcher* glowing dark-red, instead of the usual shades of gray. This effect would have been visible even to Gloria in F 004. Those who had done their homework could point out, only just to be seen, some of the other, less hospitable, planets in the Zora System, such as Kalymnos and Amorgos (although which was which?). Zora itself looked not so much red as dark-brown, which was no doubt a more reassuring and comfortable color to live with on a day-to-day basis. The Kallipygian Moons were nowhere to be seen.

Sadly, unit F 106 had no porthole window.

CHAPTER ELEVEN
GUARDIAN REBEK'A

GUARDIAN REBEK'A STOOD IN THE DOORWAY. To be accurate, her bulk completely blocked the doorway. And she didn't look at all pleased to be there.

"There has to be a good reason for calling me over here, I assume? Tell me that good reason!"

"I called you."

"You're stating the obvious, princess! Your lover boy hasn't got my number. That would be the day, that really would, when some dirty little AdPop pages me, calling me out in the middle of docking!"

Burk sensed that Milliya was very, very nervous.

"She has something that she wants to ask you—"

"Shut up, Mr. Burk, or I might just hit you. Let her do the talking."

She turned to Milliya.

"You've been rutting with him, haven't you? No, don't answer that! I don't mind, really I don't. He has his uses, and for the moment at least we need to keep him happy, don't we?"

Burk would have liked to have said something forceful like "I love her!", or even "We love each other!" The latter would have been both speculative (*did* she love him?) and very daring. Sure, male AdPops could love and admire female Guardians—from a safe and chaste distance—because what wasn't there to love and admire? The other way round, however, was taboo. It wasn't forbidden, or even *officially* discouraged. Sex went on all the time, and female Guardians were just as ruthless in enforcing the female equivalent of *droit de seigneur* as their male colleagues were in harvesting frightened female AdPops. But a female Guardian in love with a male AdPop? The idea was simply so ridiculous that it was virtually unthinkable.

When it indeed happened—as, like all ridiculous things, it occasionally did—it caused unspeakable embarrassment. The female Guardian would then be "encouraged" to give up her Guardian status, the miserable AdPop "encouraged" to apply for a posting in a distant corner of the galaxy, perhaps in an all-male mining settlement populated by convicts. Burk suspected that Guardian Rebek'a's preferred way of "encouraging" him would be more painful than that, if not indeed terminal. He therefore kept quiet, but Guardian Rebek'a seemed to have read his thoughts.

"You're wise not to say anything, Burk. Keep it for later, much later, when you get back to Terra and can tell them what their beloved Government has been up to out on the planets. *Then* you can be as eloquent, and passionate, as you like! But don't spoil it by mentioning your intimacies with Guardians. It'll be hard enough to repair your reputation over these pedophile goings-on—though I think we can probably manage that."

Then, to Milliya: "So what is it that you wanted to ask?"

"I've told him about *sqot*. Not much, because I don't know very much."

"That doesn't matter. The settlers will tell him everything he needs to know. You must keep an eye on him, while he collects information and transmits it to Terra. When I get back, our friends will arrange for your posting to be extended for as long as necessary. Then, when the storm breaks, there'll be a judicial enquiry and he'll be brought back as a witness. You'll need to guard him carefully, make sure that they don't organize a convenient 'accident' for him on the return voyage."

"Rebek'a, there's something I need to know."

Again, that familiar use of her name. Rebek'a stiffened perceptibly, the two Guardians' eyes met, and for a moment Burk felt completely excluded as some kind of emotional charge passed between them.

"I know that you've been making the beast with him—I can smell it on you, princess—but maybe you've been *talking* to him, too? A tiny bit too much, I fear! Well, then, what silly things has he been telling you, then?"

"He knew nothing. And he has learned nothing from *me*, but Colleague Adriyan spoke to him—before you killed him."

The senior Guardian smiled sardonically.

"A few minutes too late, apparently. So, what did the

little rat tell him?"

"He told him that it was the settlers who were burning and destroying the *sqot*—"

"Yes yes, as part of a Government-organized scheme, we know that."

"No! Not because of the Government. Because someone else put them up to it! Someone who wants to bring down the Government, someone with a political agenda of their own...."

"Oh, sweetheart, you're seeing conspiracies everywhere! Talk about paranoia! But I can assure you: the only conspiracy around here is that charade of turning your beloved boyfriend here into a pedophile. I had expected something more imaginative. I mean, does he *look* like one? Still, I played along with it to persuade my Guardian colleagues that I was more or less on their side. Ratty Adriyan we don't need to worry about any more. Sousanna (that stuck-up bitch!)—she's going to be a tiny bit more difficult. She's supposed to stay on Lemnos and *investigate*. Well, so be it. But our friends on the planet will find a way to keep her quiet. We must certainly make sure that she doesn't interfere with what little Burk is doing."

"Don't you see that Burk doesn't trust us? He thinks we're sending him to live with settlers who are criminals, people who'll murder him if he tries to expose what they've been doing on Lemnos!"

"That's nonsense, darling. The settlers are innocent; they were only following Government orders."

"Adriyan said otherwise. And it's his word against

ours. No, it's his word against *yours*—because I don't know anymore what to believe either."

Burk heard an emotion in her voice that he had never heard before. To his own amazement, he found himself joining in the quarrel between the two Guardians.

"No, she's right, I don't know what to believe, or whom I can trust!"

Guardian Rebek'a looked at him absolutely venomously. Burk felt his knees going. His courage evaporated at once.

"I told you to shut up, little man! If I didn't—*unfortunately*— need you, I would break you in half with my hands. *Now*. I've put up long enough with your AdPop stupidity. I've let you screw my girl—yes, you were too stupid even to work that one out! Do you think my little princess fell for you because of your manifold charms, Burk? You heap of steaming ordure! You creep! Get it into your thick AdPop head—I *sent* her to you!"

Even as Burk's whole emotional world fell apart, he noticed that Milliya was blushing, something that Burk had never seen her do before, and she was trembling. The look that she gave Burk was distraught. This was a new, unfamiliar Milliya.

"It wasn't like that, believe me! It only started that way."

"You're pathetic, both of you. Truly. But I still need you both. So: pay attention! Here's what's going to happen! Since I can't trust you, there'll need to be a change of plan. We'll have to do it a different way than

I intended. First things first, though. Sweetheart, go to the locked store-cupboard in the other room, key in the numbers "6478", open the cupboard, and bring me the large box that you'll find inside. Don't try to open the box, though. *Not yet.*"

Milliya hesitated momentarily, but then left the room to carry out her instructions. The second that she was gone, Guardian Rebek'a turned on Burk.

"Don't think that I don't know what you've been doing to my princess, down to every sordid little detail! I can imagine it all, because *I've* been there too. Except—there are things that she likes, that I *taught* her to like, that you won't know about. She'd be ashamed if you did. And I think that's sweet: girls should have their little secrets, don't you agree?"

The look that she gave Burk was more expressive of evil than any he had seen on her face—including how she had looked as she murdered Guardian Adriyan— since the spiteful gaze she had fixed on him when he was first brought for interrogation.

Milliya returned, carrying a large rectangular container.

"Put it down on the table. I'm going to show you what's inside, and then I'm going to tell you about it: the truth, the whole truth, and nothing but the truth. I owe you that, princess, although to be quite honest you don't really *need* to know. Your boyfriend here *does*, however, because, as I said, there's been a change of plan. And from now on, you'll both do what I say. OK? There'll be no philosophical arguments about right or wrong—you'll just do what you're told. Now" (to Burk) "go over and unlatch the lid, open it, and hand me some of what you find inside."

Milliya stepped forward.

"Stop! Before he goes and puts his hands inside, tell me what it is! Is it dangerous? And why are you asking *him* to do this, and not me?"

"He'll be quite safe, your precious little AdPop. Don't worry, there's nothing dangerous in the box. It's *sqot*, darling. That's all. It won't bite him. It's time for you both to finally make its acquaintance!"

CHAPTER TWELVE

SQOT

BURK OPENED THE BOX AS HE HAD BEEN INSTRUCTED. He pushed back the lid and looked inside. The stuff inside looked very peculiar. It was a dull green color, with patches of brown, and seemed to be completely inert, but there was something about it that suggested to Burk that it might be organic, and capable of movement.

"Go ahead, little man."

Rather gingerly, Burk lowered his hand towards the *sqot*. Should he try to scoop some of it out with his fingers? Or maybe pinch the surface together and then break off a piece? As he was considering what to do next, the surface of his hand must have come closer to the surface of the *sqot*, because it seemed to shudder slightly, with a ripple of changing color moving across it. Burk pulled his hand away.

"Oh!"

Guardian Rebek'a laughed nastily.

"Yes, it's alive. And it reacts to what it senses. It doesn't know that you're harmless, little Burk. Go on, pinch a bit of it together with your fingers and lift it up."

"I don't want to."

"I wasn't *asking* you. Do it!"

It cost Burk a considerable effort to do as she ordered. As he lowered his hand towards the *sqot*, this time more intentionally, it juddered perceptibly. He tried half-heartedly to scoop some of it up, if necessary by breaking it off first, and was amazed to find some of the *sqot* slipping (or sliding?) easily into his hand. *It had somehow parted from the rest of its own accord.* How could that be? There it was in the palm of his hand—and it was now a bright green, and vibrating.

"*Pulsate* was the word that my ratty deceased friend used, I believe? Quite an accurate description, I would say."

"But it's alive!"

"Oh yes. That's one of the wonders of the galaxy that you have there in your grubby paw. You shouldn't keep it in a box, of course—it doesn't like that at all—but I just couldn't resist. I have my own little *sqot* to play with. And now you've woken it up good and proper."

"But it changed color. And look," (he was amazed once again) "look! It's *still* changing color!"

"Doesn't your face change color as your emotions change, Burk? Angry red, sickly green, frightened white? And what can you *feel*, holding it in your hand?"

"It's kind of, I don't know: shifting?"

He struggled to find the right word.

"Forming? Re-forming itself?"

"Exactly, Burk! Or, alternatively, perhaps it isn't."

"What do you mean? It's alive, isn't it?"

Milliya joined in: "I know what it is—it's reacting to changes in his body temperature! No, I've got it—it's ultra-sensitively aware of his emotional state!"

"It, it, it, darlings! But why should it be an 'it'? Why not a 'they'?"

"I don't understand, Rebek'a."

"There are more things in heaven and earth, Horatio—"

"—than are dreamt of in your philosophy!"

This time Guardian Rebek'a's smile was almost amiable (though not quite).

"Ah, Burk, what would we do without our brilliant graduate in Media Studies, minor in *Literature*?"

She turned to Milliya.

"Your AdPop dimwit can't tell shit from butter, but *you* should be able to. That is an alien life form that he's got there in his hand, agreed?"

She didn't wait for a reply. Her attention was now focused entirely on Milliya, but even if Burk had felt brave enough to attack her, he was still holding the *sqot*, and agonizingly aware that it was morphing and re-metabolizing in his hand.

"Is it an animal, or is it vegetation? We don't know. Those are Terran concepts, my dear. Those are *our* categories. Why does an alien creature have to have a head, a face, limbs? Why does it have to be about the same size as we are? You remember those ridiculous twentieth-century entertainments, I'm sure—"

"Science fiction."

"Burk no doubt deconstructed them in some pathetic

undergraduate class. The filmed versions had human actors wearing grotesque makeup and costumes, but you could always see that it was a Terran underneath. They had to be like that, though, because Terrans can't conceive of Otherness except as a version of themselves. Like those Europeans who discovered the Americas, wittering on about the Noble Savage or the Garden of Eden..."

"But they still wiped them out, didn't they?"

"Oh, little Burk, Colleague Adriyan was right after all! You're a bloody Ciaranite, you've been imbibing poor Dr. Burke's sentimental tosh about the 'aboriginal peoples'. Just joking! I doubt whether you have the brain-power. But let me tell you this: the Other is not like us; it doesn't have our best interests at heart, oh no; and when we encounter it, the best thing we can do is wipe it out as quickly as we can. Before it does the same to us."

She paused.

"Incidentally, that's the Other that you're holding there in your hand. I hope it likes you!"

Burk moved to put the *sqot* back into the box—who could tell what it might do to him?—but Guardian Rebek'a signaled to him to stop.

"Animal, vegetable: who cares? They're *our* categories. What about 'it' and 'they'? Do you think that that *sqot* in your hand has a name? Even if you knew how to ask it?"

"Rebek'a, they must have done some research before they started destroying it, surely?"

"Oh yes, princess, we may not completely under-stand its language, but we do know that it communi-cates in a very sophisticated way. Or rather: that *they* communicate."

"What do you mean: 'it' or 'they'?"

"Ask your friend Burk how many *sqot* he has in his hand!"

Burk spoke up before Milliya could repeat the question.

"You know that I can't tell! It's like a handful of...I don't know what. Jellyfish? No, maybe not."

"Is it one *sqot*?"

"No, I pulled it away from the rest. It could be *part* of one, I suppose."

"Like a detached limb, perhaps? But I think you'll find that any part that you had removed would behave like the *sqot* in your hand. And what you are holding is capable of anything that the *sqot* still left in the box can do."

"So how many of them are there, Rebek'a?"

"How many do you want? How many do you need? How many do *they* need? You see, my dear, these ideas that we have about 'individuals' and 'groups' are *our* concepts. We may say that we love each other," (Burk winced) "that we 'think as one', but of course we never do. *Sqot* does, though, quite genuinely."

"But you said that it communicates, so there must be individual members communicating with each other?"

"Maybe. Maybe not. There is certainly informa-tion circulating. There is a communication system.

We know that *sqot* is intelligent (as we would define intelligence) and that it can do different things, and carry out different functions, some of them potentially dangerous to us."

"For instance?"

"Princess, you know that I couldn't possibly reveal that information, even if we didn't have your toyboy listening in. By the way: keep holding that stuff, Burk! I have a treat in store for you, if you're a good lad!"

"Then *sqot* is something like a swarm of bees, or an antheap, but without a queen?"

"Not bad—you'll make it to Grade II eventually! But 'antheap' isn't quite right. We can break *sqot* down into physiological components, but we don't know whether these have any consistent characteristics, or clearly defined, permanent functions. All we know is that 'it' forms patterns of individuals, with separate functions, according to what is required, and that these patterns shift all the time. That is what you are experiencing right now, Burk, with the *sqot* in your hand. That is what the changing color, the undulating, is all about."

"The pulsating is an individual *sqot*, then, expressing itself?"

"Well done, Burk. I see that you have the capacity to remember new words of more than one syllable after all! But the pulsating—difficult word, that!—is something very complex. It's—communication. *Sqot* reshapes itself constantly according to what is needed. One part of it realizes that there's a situation that requires action, and so it tells the rest by conveying its feeling that something needs to be done! They don't communicate information, they communicate emotions. *Sqot* is totally in tune; 'the community is a unity'. (That's good, I must remember that!) There are no individuals, because they don't need to be different all the time, only when they're reacting to situations, when they need to take on different roles."

She thought for a moment.

"Like a choir where the members can all sing different parts and descants, but to no pre-arranged pattern (anyone can sing anything at any time), and they make it up as they go along."

"So what's the *sqot* in my hand doing?"

"What do you think? It's not trying to make love to you, I'm sure!"

"It's frightened, Rebek'a."

"Oh yes, but you saw the way that it detached itself and slipped into his hand? It was sacrificing itself for the rest, drawing your wicked Burk away from the rest of the stuff in the box."

"And the colors?"

"It's sending information—or rather feelings—to what's in the box. Relief? Fear? Satisfaction? Warning? Encouragement? Who knows? Our scientists could probably find that out. If Burk walked out of this unit, far enough for the *sqot* in his hand to be out of transmitting range, it would die. But I don't know what that distance would be. It would be interesting to find out!"

Burk looked at the *sqot* in amazement, and was about to say something, but Milliya was quicker.

"Why didn't the *sqot* that you stole and brought back to Terra, the *sqot* that you've got in that box, die then?"

"Because, princess, I seem by accident to have found the critical mass—quite a modest amount, actually—needed for an independent colony of the stuff. Oh, what a waste of my talents, I should have been a researcher!"

As Guardian Rebek'a was smugly congratulating herself, the sound and light signals of the unit went on.

"Disembarking time, I would say. From this point on, you're both going to do exactly as you're told. Princess—you are going to *leave*. You'll be on Lemnos, as arranged, keeping an eye on bloody golden girl Sousanna. Take your case and go. Hurry, or you'll miss the shuttle!"

But Milliya made no move to leave.

"Burk—you are going to *stay*. You will be coming back to Terra with me to tell blood-curdling stories of colonial exploitation, of intelligent species being wiped out, that'll destroy the Government. First, I'll have to suppress the pedophile smear. You won't mind that, will you? (You can still bugger little boys in your spare time if you want to—just keep it out of the media.) And I'll have to protect my star witness carefully. There will be people in the Government who won't want you to tell your story."

"My story?"

"Which will be what I tell you to say, Burk. No fear, you'll have plenty of time on the return voyage to learn it off by heart—and when the big day comes, I'll be right behind you to make sure that you say it properly! And one false move from *either* of you, and the other will be seriously and painfully hurt. You got it? It's a cleverly symmetrical arrangement, isn't it? For an improvised plan, not bad at all! Based entirely on the idea of *love*—that both of you love each each other so much that you'll behave. I didn't realize that I believed in love…. Well, well, Rebek'a! You never cease to amaze me: you're a romantic!"

Burk made no move either. He wasn't sure what to do with the *sqot* in his hand—could he just transfer it back to the box, as simple as that?—though there was another, even more convincing, argument for not moving: Guardian Rebek'a had drawn her taser and was pointing it at him.

"I'm beginning to lose my patience with both of you. Princess, *it's time to go.*"

Milliya sought Burk's eyes.

"Darling, she's crazy, but we can stop her if we do it together. If we jump her together. She looks big. She looks dangerous. But she always gets a reaction from the pods, I know that. Her balance is not good. She's still groggy. It's worth a try."

"Milliya!"

It was the first time that Burk had heard the Guardian use Milliya's name.

"Don't be foolish!"

"Then stop this. I don't want to have to hurt you. I owe you so much."

There was no response. Milliya turned to Burk.

"We can do this! Don't worry about the *sqot*: it won't do anything to hinder you when you move, I'm sure of it. It hates her. And she won't fire her taser at you. She won't risk it—she needs you alive and fit on Terra. She's got a Government to bring down."

Pause.

"And she won't shoot at me either," her voice dropped to a whisper: "for a different reason."

Guardian Rebek'a took a step backward. For a moment, she seemed to be in shock, but then she laughed.

"Oh, you're good. You're *good*. Your cards are crap, but you're still playing to win. You've got the makings of a Guardian leader, princess! But this time it's not going to work, is it? I've set the taser to 'Low', and it'll only put him to sleep for a few minutes. And, groggy or not, I think I can still handle you, my dear, even with the proverbial hand tied behind my back."

"I think she's right, Milliya. I'll go back to Terra and do what she wants. Maybe it'll even do some good. If there's a scandal, it might save the last of the *sqot*."

Guardian Rebek'a grinned at them both, and then laughed out loud.

"Only an AdPop drone with a literature degree, but he's still got some sense in his head! But you won't save any *sqot*, little Burk! That's the beauty of all this. Two birds with one stone. It'll finish off the Government, but only after *debates*, and *commissions of enquiry*, and *legal challenges*, and you name it whatever else. They'll fight to the bitter end to save their skins. And while they're doing it, my settler friends will polish off what's left of the green gunk, and good riddance too!"

Burk felt the *sqot* in his hand shifting and pulsating.

"But I've saved the best till last. I did promise you a treat, Burk, and now it's coming. Milliya: go to the other room and fetch the salt dispenser from the table. Go on, do it now—or I might decide to hurt your little friend, so that he can't give you a goodbye kiss when you leave in a couple of minutes from now!"

The *sqot* was now moving with an intense rhythmic shudder, like a stuttering transportation engine on a Terran country road. It seemed to be sweating, or liquefying, too.

Milliya returned with the salt dispenser and placed it on the side-table.

"I said that my settler friends will polish off the last of the *sqot* and, do you know what, they'll enjoy it too! I'll let you into a little secret. It tastes good! No—it tastes *fantastic*. Like ambrosia, the food of the gods. Not the way the first settlers ate it, of course. They thought you could eat it like fruit off a tree, or cook it like green cabbage. You do eat it raw, but there's a little trick you need to know."

Her eyes gleamed.

"First, you make it aware that you're going to eat it, and let that sink in for a few moments. It doesn't like that at all, and it shits itself! It exudes a slimy liquid, like thick balsamic vinegar, perhaps a pain relief, something like human endomorphins? Then you sprinkle some ordinary household salt on it, and you wait a few seconds. The salt reacts with the slimy stuff, there's some interesting biochemistry, and the *sqot* turns into a delicious, god-like mush!"

"You're sick, Rebek'a. That's evil."

"You're such an innocent, princess! Why do you think I carried a whole box of the stuff with me, to Terra and back, and kept it hidden from everyone? For scientific analysis? For research? For experiments? No! *Because it tastes good!* And I do swear—it could even be addictive too…. Good that we're going to eradicate what's left of it!"

She turned to Burk.

"Now comes your treat. You're going to taste *sqot*, you lucky boy—"

"No!"

"Oh yes you are. Because if you don't, I shall taser the little lady, somewhere where it'll cause her exquisite pain. How about a taser burn on the breast? We'll take the left one, I think, it's slightly bigger than the right, as you'll no doubt have noticed… Come on, Burk! Be a man for just once in your life! You've got the muck in your hand. I can see from here that it's already crapped itself. So we're already halfway there. Look, there's the salt, use it. You don't realize how much I'm spoiling you, Burk—you're joining an élite club of connoisseurs. This is the most wonderful taste experience the human race has ever been offered. *Enjoy!* It's like eating a kiss. Or a scream. Or both at the same time."

Then something happened.

CHAPTER THIRTEEN
THE UNIVERSE IS A
DANGEROUS PLACE

WHAT HAPPENED? Everyone participated, everyone—
Burk, Milliya, Guardian Rebek'a, the *sqot*—contrib-
uted to the result, but it would be difficult to understand
it without a recording, an image, of some kind. Was
it *caused*? By a single actant, or by a combination of
their actions? Was it *orchestrated* (an idea that Burk
later in his life found increasingly convincing)?

If the events were unclear, their result was immediately evident: Guardian Rebek'a lying unconscious on
the floor, bleeding slightly from a head wound caused
presumably by contact with the edge of the side-table.

But how had this come about? Milliya and Burk had
indeed both moved suddenly, to "jump" her, actions
that would not normally have been predicated as very
likely to succeed, except by a miraculously precise
degree of coordination. Guardian Rebek'a had in
response carried out a ruthless and deadly martial arts
move that, ninety-nine times out of a hundred, would
have incapacitated both her attackers. These elements
made up a sequence, or a tableau, that should not have

led to the result that it did, but which had somehow been re-arranged to do precisely that.

The timing of Milliya's and Burk's movements had been impeccable, as if orchestrated, and, in the vital fraction of a second that mattered most, Guardian Rebek'a had slipped, on the slimy handful of *sqot* that was now on the floor, and fallen, her head hitting the table on the way down. But what was the *sqot* doing there? Burk had neither dropped it nor thrown it.

Milliya was the first to react. She read off a message that was coming through on the personal communicator attached to her wrist.

"'Markko Mann' and 'Guardian Jo-anna' can still make the shuttle. They miscalculated the time window for the transfer flights, so the first shuttle craft has only just left. That gives us at least an hour. But—what are we going to do with her? She could wake up at any moment?"

"You could reset her taser and knock her out for a few hours, the way they did with me?"

There was faintest sound of human movement behind them.

"Or you could kill her!"

Neither of them had heard him enter, but now the little Scribe Jacoob stood there, looking from one of them to the other.

"She deserves to die. Do to her what she did to her colleague Adriyan. Reset it to 'HIGH' and taser her to oblivion!"

It was strange to hear the hunched little man speak

so forcefully. For a moment there was silence.

"No. I couldn't do that to her" (this was addressed less to the Scribe than to Burk) "whatever she may have done."

"I know. Nor could I. We should stun her properly, and then leave her here. We'll be on Lemnos before she comes to."

"My dear Mr. Burk, are you really so certain? And what if they should find her, and manage to revive her, while you are still on the control vessel, or on the shuttle? Are you both willing to take that risk?"

"Yes" (from both of them, spontaneously).

"You're kind and well-meaning people. I'm not a cruel man, truly I'm not, but sometimes historical processes—*progressive* processes—demand a personal sacrifice from us. You know what I mean? The eggs you break to make the omelet?"

Milliya: "The answer is till 'no'."

Burk: "You're a Ciaranite, aren't you? That's the way *they* talk! So you're an enemy of the Government, just like she is."

The little Scribe smiled, surprisingly sweetly.

"But for very different reasons, Mr. Burk. You know what she represents," he pointed to the Guardian's still comatose form, "and what she would do with *sqot*. By the way, I think you should pick it up, Mr. Burk, it is after all an intelligent living creature, and return it to the rest of the *sqot*, wherever that is—"

Burk did just that.

"—Thank you! And I regard the label 'Ciaranite'

as highly flattering, although it's not a word I would personally use. What you might not know, Mr. Burk, is that there is a broader context here: a *conspiracy* to overthrow the elected Government, and replace it with the, er, *non-elected* Imperial Advisory Council. That is where this lady's friends are to be found, and they are the ones who would like to rule the universe. All in the name of the Emperor, of course."

"Did you know this, Milliya?"

"Not directly. But I've met some of them, and I know what that would mean for all of us."

"Then we should go to the Government with this, straight away! We could speak to Guardian Sousanna."

"Whoa, whoa! That's what they used to shout at horses, incidentally. Have you ever seen a horse? No matter. Please remember this, Mr. Burk: Guardian Sousanna is a brave and intelligent person, but she is also a Government servant, and she has ambitions of her own. Don't forget: she was prepared to send you back to Terra in disgrace on a trumped-up charge, was she not? Merely to save the Government from embarrassment."

"Then they know what is happening to *sqot*?"

"Yes, and her brief is to find out who is behind the destruction, and eliminate them. Sooner or later she will identify this lady here as one of the culprits, and take appropriate measures."

"Then we're on the same side!"

"Oh Mr. Burk, if only the Government shared just a little of your idealism. But there is wickedness there, too—evil, selfish people who have their own agenda for *sqot*. They want to research the biochemistry of the stuff, use what they find to try and create a docile, cooperative society, everyone pulling together, selflessly! But for whose benefit? The happy, brain-dead masses would still be ruled by an élite, and I'm sure you can guess who *they* would be! It's not a scheme that would work, though. What *might* work, however, is this: they've heard about the addictiveness of *sqot*-eating, so—they factory-farm it, and use it as a 'happy drug' to keep the Terrans under total control."

"That's disgusting!"

"No, my lady, it's not disgusting. It's *sinister*. So— might I suggest that we do the tasering *now*, while she's still quiet? Perhaps you would do the honors?"

Milliya retrieved the taser from where it had fallen and carefully reset the controls. It was a state-of-the-art weapon with multiple settings. It had been set to "Low", which would only have sedated Guardian Rebek'a for five or ten minutes. To knock her out for a couple of hours, making allowance for her massive physique and strength, would require a setting like "Medium" or "High Sedation", which would possibly kill someone older and smaller like Scribe Jacoob, for instance. Milliya didn't want to take that risk, but the Scribe insisted.

Milliya held the taser as steadily as she could, activated it and pumped a high sedative dose into the body of the older woman.

They couldn't leave her in F 106. It was faintly

conceivable that some of the Level F units might be allocated to passengers for the return voyage.

Then Jacoob made a suggestion: why not deposit her in one of the large waste bins built into the walls of the outer gangways? Most of these were full to bursting with junk abandoned by the would-be settlers, but the bin nearest to F 106 conveniently had nothing but unwanted clothes in it and was half-empty. Perhaps F 106 hadn't been the only unit being used for temporary and surreptitious purposes in that part of the ship! The bins wouldn't be emptied out into space until the *Starstretcher* had left the Zora System—that was standard Galactic Navigational Law.

Guardian Rebek'a would be quite comfortable for a few hours on a pile of abandoned coats and undergarments, and when she came to the bin was low enough for her to be able to climb out of it unaided. All that remained was to wait for an all-clear from Jacoob, and Burk and Milliya then carried out what looked like a huge, rolled-up carpet (and partly was) and with a supreme effort heaved it into the waste bin.

The time had now come for Burk and Milliya to head for the disembarkation point. The Scribe would not be going with them on the shuttle—his hope to be allowed to go down to the surface of Lemnos for sightseeing had not been fulfilled, but he might still be able to buy the crystals and colored dust for his grandchildren in the tourist shop in the outer hall of the control vessel. And he would be entrusted with the box of *sqot*. Now that *would* be something to show his grandchildren! In the end, of course, it would have to be returned to Lemnos.

Milliya disappeared for a few minutes to change her clothes and freshen up. The moment that she was gone, the little Scribe pressed his face close to Burk's and whispered: "Listen!"

He led Burk to a corner of the room where he had a clear view of both the outer door of F 106 and the door through which Milliya had just disappeared.

"Listen well, Mr. Burk. You'll never hear anything as important as this again in your whole life, I promise you that! I haven't told you the whole story, but this is now for your ears only."

"And Milliya?"

"She's a Guardian—and I don't trust them. If *you* want to trust her, that's your decision, and be it on your own head. But it's your risk."

"Very well."

"Mr. Burk: you know that there was an *incident* on this ship?"

"There was some business or other…perhaps a pirate attack?"

"No. You know that that can't be true."

He paused, as if not sure how to continue.

"*Mr. Burk, we are not alone in the universe.* And I don't mean *sqot*, or ferns. Two planetary settlements have been wiped out, with ruthless cruelty. And several ships of the Imperial Fleet have been attacked. No-one knows who or what they are. They come out of the depths of space and disappear back into it. They have no name. The Fleet Commanders call them 'the Outsiders', and they want their friends on the Imperial Advisory Council to mobilize for war. The Government are terrified that when the media get hold of this—that the Empire is *unsafe*—there will be panic. No-one will volunteer for the settlements anymore—"

"Just as Terra itself is becoming uninhabitable."

"Exactly. So you know what this means? They'll need to have greater control over the population. Soon it's just going to be about *power*, and nothing else. Do you see now why the Government is so interested in *sqot*?"

But before Burk could respond, Milliya reappeared and insisted that they should go. They would not be traveling together, she said, but it would be convenient if they could at least be on the same shuttle.

Once on the surface of Lemnos, they would have to go underground. Guardian Rebek'a's settler friends were waiting to help them, yes, sure, but that was no longer an option. They would need to find new friends and allies now. And ways for Burk to transfer whatever he discovered about the "Great *sqot* Scandal", as it would no doubt come to be known, back to his contacts on Terra.

Burk could barely pay attention to what she was saying, so violent were the thoughts and images that were now circulating in his mind. But she managed to bundle him, and their small cases, out of the unit and along the mostly deserted gangways of Level F as far as the place where they separated, he taking a staircase, she walking on to find a lift. If possible, they should not be seen together, here, on the control vessel, or on the shuttle. The Scribe had already quietly detached himself from them and disappeared.

Burk had experienced a magical moment of empathy, of emotional communication, with *sqot*. It was unique and wonderful, and must be saved! Humankind had miserably failed to preserve the other higher life-forms on Terra, except those that it took for meat or as pets. What had the gorillas been like? Or the dolphins? Burk and Milliya must now take on the double task of saving what was left of *sqot* from the settlers, while learning more about it. *Befriending* it, even. Could *sqot* perhaps be a useful ally for the Terrans against this mysterious new enemy?

Had Burk but known it, Milliya was also brooding over *sqot*. Her thoughts were going in a different direction, though. Could *sqot* be trusted? It spread so easily—only a small amount was needed to set up a colony—and it was so much more focused and united in its will than humans ever were. It could turn out to be an insatiable weed, an unstoppable virus.

Sunk in thought as they were, neither of them realized that other passengers were for a few moments enjoying one of the greatest sights of the universe. The two Kallipygian moons of Lemnos had after all decided to come out to play. Catching the light of Zora at different angles, they seemed to be trapped in a kind of visual dialog with each other, but shimmering with gorgeous colors never seen in the smoggy atmosphere of Terra. And, as if in response, Lemnos had lost its gray-brown dullness. Its surface, while not predominantly green, now gleamed, as though wet, in an array of colors sown with twinkling points of light. On the control vessel, those lucky enough to be near a porthole, or even on a viewing platform, reacted with "oohs" and "aahs". Burk and Milliya hurried on to join them, unaware of what they were missing.

* * * * * * *

ON THE CONTROL DECK OF THE *STARSTRETCHER*, two wary junior officers watched the Commander finalizing arrangements for the ship to shed itself of the control vessel before setting off on the long return voyage to Terra. The new settlers (and a handful of tourists, Guardians and AdPop technicians) had been disembarked, new passengers had been welcomed on board, and some interesting items of freight had been loaded, as well as assorted edible provisions, the modest produce of the plantations of Lemnos; no Goro-nuts, however.

The Commander was absorbed in his work, but visibly irritated. The docking had gone well, and it had been pleasant to meet up with an old colleague once more. Yet there must be something on his mind, for him to be so agitated. Maybe it was the uncertainties that might face them on the return journey; maybe it was only the fact that the ceremonial hamper of Goro-nuts (and the products made from them, including the renowned whiskey), a presentation gift that he had been much looking forward to, had failed to materialize. Whatever the cause might be, the two young officers could see that he wasn't in a good mood and they were understandably reluctant to pester him over a trifle.

"Did you actually hear him say that the waste bins should be emptied at T-speed?"

"No, not in so many words, but there is a signed order."

"Yes, but it's against Galactic Navigational Law, isn't it? If we pump it out now, the stuff will all go into orbit round Lemnos. What a junkyard it'll be—the settlers will be truly grateful for that! You know there are good reasons why ships always empty their bins in interstellar space, well away from the planets, the first time that they slow down."

"*Well, maybe we're not going to slow down on the way back!* Anyhow, that's what the order says, look. He signed it days ago. All the rubbish gets chucked out the moment we set off. At T-speed. See? There's his signature, and it's signed and dated by the Scribe Jacoob, the little hunchback. Everything as it should be."

"Well, one of them will know what he's doing. Won't he?"

APPENDIX ONE
TERRAN SOCIAL STRATA

Guardian V—Senior leadership
Guardian IV—Junior leadership
Guardian III—Officers
Guardian II—Non-commissioned officers
Guardian I—Rank and file
Useful population (UsePop)—Made up of "breeders" (f) and their "consorts" (m)
Additional population (AdPop)—Made up of "ladies" (f) and "drones" (m)
Surplus population (SurPop)—Underclass, convicts, criminals, addicts, social undesirables

APPENDIX TWO
INTERSTELLAR TRANSPORTATION

Transportation speeds

T-speed—Terrestrial speed
S-speed—Slide hyperdrive
HS-speed—High slide (requiring transportation pods for everyone except highly trained, selected personnel)
VHS-speed—Very high slide (transportation pods required for everyone)

Types of ship

Freighter—T, S
Priority freighter—T, S, HS
People transporter—T, S, HS
Battle cruiser—T, S, HS
Fighter—T, S, HS
Courier ship—T, S, HS, VHS

ABOUT THE AUTHOR

FRANCIS JARMAN was born in Germany, but brought up and educated in England. According to family tradition, he is descended from the Thracian slave Androcles (of *Androcles and the Lion* fame). Dr. Jarman teaches comparative cultural studies and intercultural communication at the University of Hildesheim (Germany), but has also taught or lectured in Belgium, Bulgaria, Cyprus, Denmark, Egypt, England, Finland, Greece, India, Italy, Japan, Lithuania, Malta, Poland, Portugal, Spain, and Thailand. A playwright, novelist, and classical numismatist, he has on his travels met a goddess, danced in public with eunuchs, stroked a lion, sat on a snake, encountered sacred rats—and been attacked by a pig, arrested by a military patrol, and involved in the hold-up of a train by bandits (although none of these events have appeared so far in his fiction).

www.ingramcontent.com/pod-product-compliance
Lightning Source LLC
Chambersburg PA
CBHW020653180626
46816CB00003B/1256